UNBOUND

A NOVEL IN VERSE

BY ANN E. BURG

SCHOLASTIC INC.

PART

ONE

When Mama tells me
I'm goin
to the Big House,
she makes me promise
to always be good,
to listen to the Missus
n never talk back,
to lower my eyes
n say, *Yes, ma'am,*
no, ma'am,
n to not speak
less spoken to first.

She tells me bout
the new dress
I'm sure to get—
n sweet muffins
every mornin,
she says,
pullin the thread
from Thomas's
old baby gown.

I wind the limp thread
round a stick, slow
n careful so not to break it.
I like soft clothes
n sweet muffins,
but not if it means
leavin Mama.

Since I was little,
Mama's been tellin me,
You keep those eyes
lookin up—
that's where the good Lord
n His angels live.

So how come now
she's changin her mind?

Promise you'll keep
your eyes down, she says.

I promise.

Promise you'll keep
your mouth closed.

I promise.

Promise you won't
talk back.
Promise you'll
keep your
thoughts n questions
bou—

n suddenly,
like a clap of thunder
in a sweet blue sky,
all my promisin

starts feelin like
a fistful of thorns
is scratchin my brain.

I promise. I promise—
n then
CRACK!

I drop to the dirt floor
n crunch into a ball.

I won't go! I say.
I want to stay with you!

Aunt Sara stands
in the cabin doorway.
Willy's playin with the hem
of her dress,
n she's holdin Thomas
in her arms.
Mama shoos em away
n kneels down.
She tugs me apart
n takes me into her arms.
I pull away.

I won't go, I cry.
I won't leave Uncle Jim
n his night stories,
or the sound
of his soft singin
when he tends
our moonlight garden.

I won't go. I kick.
I won't leave
little Thomas n Willy.
Aunt Sara's old.
She can sing to em
when Mama works
in the fields, but
who'll stand over em
wavin a dried leaf
to give em a breeze
when they nap?

Who'll play with em
n chase em
into a lump of giggles
when they wake?

I won't go! I won't go!

I pound n thrash,
scream n stomp.

I WON'T GO!
I WANT TO STAY
WITH YOU!

Mama wraps
her arms
tight round mine.

My sweet baby child,
she whispers.
My sweet baby child.

The wetness on her face
mingles with my tears—
n tastes like blood.

Uncle Jim says Mama's
the prettiest mama in the county.
Her arms n legs may be bony
as kindlin, he says, laughin,
but she's got the softest eyes
n the kindest heart.

I wish I had soft brown eyes
like Mama's, n skin
what's dark n smooth like hers,
stead of light blue eyes
n pale skin.

Well, Grace,
you have my curls,
Mama always says,
kissin my hair.
My baby's beautiful
jus the way she is.

Mama tries to be cheery
even when she's tired.
Aunt Sara says that's cause
the good Lord
put Mama on this earth
to remind folks
there's still goodness in the world.
I agree n Uncle Jim does too.

Uncle Jim is Thomas n Willy's daddy.
I don't have a daddy.

Course, Aunt Sara says
everybody's got a daddy—
I jus never laid eyes on mine.
I never heared him sing
or feeled him liftin me to the moon
n laughin like Uncle Jim does
with Willy n Thomas.

It's my Aunt Sara
what's been helpin Mama
take care of me
since I was a baby.
She's not really my aunt,
but Mama says
the folks what love you,
what hold you
n soothe you,
what worry bout you
n make sure you's clothed n fed,
Mama says,
these folks is your family.

She says Uncle Jim's my daddy
in all the ways what count.
I only call him Uncle Jim
cause that's what I called him
before he jumped the broom
n married my mama.

Mama says we got two days
before I leave for the Big House.
Says it's no use
stampin our feet or cryin.
Says there's things we can change
n things we can't.

You's only goin up the hill,
she says, smilin.
But her voice quivers,
n a sorrowin tear clings
to her bottom lash.

Up the hill don't seem far,
but Master Allen lives
up the hill,
n if you cross Master Allen,
he might send you away
like he sent away Uncle John.

Uncle John was an old man
what worked in the fields.
Iron chains stretched
cross his feet
so he couldn't hardly lift his legs.

Mama told me Uncle John
got caught runnin
one-too-many times.
Master Allen was tired
of chasin him
so durin the day,
he locked Uncle John's ankles
in iron circles,
n when nighttime came,
he chained Uncle John
to his bed.

Only you can't weed
tobacco fields
in iron chains
so finally Master Allen
brought Uncle John
to the auction block.

Uncle Jim says
the auction block's
a putrid place
where folks is
pulled n poked,

prodded n paraded
jus like they's a prize heifer.
You hear auction, n you run,
he says.
Auction's nothin
but weepin mamas,
whimperin children,
n the callous voice
what calls out numbers
n makes commands.
Lift that shirt.
Roll those pants.

There's some words
what make my bones shiver,
n *auction*'s one of em.

How'm I goin to live
in the Master's house?

What if I cross him
n he sends me
to the auction block?

Aunt Sara mus be worryin
bout this too
cause the next mornin
when the horn sounds
n Mama n Uncle Jim
leave for the fields,
she tells me I got some
listenin to do before
I start my chores.

Aunt Sara's shriveled
n skinny
as a dried tobacco leaf,
but her voice snaps
like fresh-cut pine knots
what's throwed in the fire.
*Your mama don't want
to scare you,* she says,
*but don't be thinkin
times is soft in the Big House.
Don't be imaginin
fancy clothes n sweet muffins.*

Aunt Sara's eyes flash.
*Master Allen'll be worryin
bout his tobacco,
but the Missus'll be watchin you,
jus watchin n waitin for you
to look cross-eyed
or make a mistake.*

Aunt Sara lowers her voice
n the flint in her eyes
fades into thin, crusty slits.

Don't know why,
but the Missus
is hateful as a toad.
Nobody wants to scare you,
but you need to keep the promises
you made to your mama.

Aunt Sara don't usually
talk so much
less she's tellin me
I don't do enough
to help Mama,
so I know she's meanin
what she says.

I'll keep my promises, I say.

Aunt Sara smiles sadly,
brushin her rough, gnarly fingers
gainst my face.

I wish I could run away.

Willy wakes up,
starts pokin Thomas,
n before long, they's
chasin, crawlin, n climbin
like baby squirrels.

While Aunt Sara
gives the boys breakfast—
a scantlin of cornmeal
n molasses—
I finish rollin the beds
n sweepin out the spiders
n chinch bugs
what got lost
lookin for a place to stay.

Me n Willy go outside
n I set him lookin
for leafhoppers
while I weed the garden.

Aunt Sara sits on her chair
mendin whatever
her knotty fingers
can still mend.
Thomas stays with her.
*This little one needs
peace,* she says.
*Sometimes our Willy's
jus too wild.*

The midday horn sounds.

I'm happy folks in the field
is finally stoppin to eat,
but time's passin too quick.

My mind's goin to break
tryin to figure a way
to stay with Mama.

When the garden's
nothin but hills n sprouts
with not a single weed,
Willy climbs on my back
like always.
We run n bounce till
there's no more breath
left inside me.
Willy's still squealin—
More, more—
but I put him down
n he starts pullin his ear
n whinin,
so I know it's naptime.

Aunt Sara gives the boys
a bit more cornmeal,
n this time,
we have some too.

I put the boys to rest
on they lumpy rags,
n Thomas falls right asleep.
But even with my best fannin
n sweetest singin,
it takes a long while
for Willy to settle.
By the time he does,
Aunt Sara's got her eyes
closed too.

I rinse our bowls
in the wash bucket
n make some mud
to patch the holes
in the wall
what make ghosty sounds
when we's tryin to sleep.

When I finish
pilin wood
for the night's cookin fire,
the boys wake.

We go outside
to play a hidin game,
cept Willy don't know
how to hide,
n Thomas cries
when I disappear behind
the cabin.

I take him in my arms
n we sit on the ground
rockin.
Willy rests his head
on my back
n a sadness what's heavier'n
a bucket of rainwater
settles inside me.

Who is goin to chase away
the ghosty winds
what blow through
cracked walls?
Who is goin to give
horsey rides
n play our hidin games?

Aunt Sara calls to us.

We cook our corn cakes
in the fire,
brush off the ashes,
n have our supper.

My heart feels like it's
goin to break in two.

Mama n Uncle Jim
don't come back to the cabin
till after dark.
The boys is sleepin again,
but me n Aunt Sara
been waitin.

Aunt Sara don't say
nothin more
bout the Big House
or the Missus,
but what she don't say
hangs heavy between us.

Mama takes me in her arms,
n before she can say anythin,
I start cryin out the tears
what's been buildin inside me.

Why can't I stay
with you forever?
I want to stay
with you forever!

Mama wraps
her skinny arms
round me
n rocks.
Back n forth
on the dirt floor
of our cabin we sway.

My sweet baby child, she says,
our forever won't start
till we get ourselves to heaven.

I wonder why the good Lord
made heaven so far away.

The next day when
the mornin horn sounds,
I overhear Mama
tell Uncle Jim
it's my light skin
what got me called
to the Big House.

All day,
while I weed the garden
n patch the walls,
while I chase the boys
n pile the wood,
Mama's words
circle in my brain.

By the time
I brush the ashes
off our corn cakes,
I got a plan.

I need some ponderin time,
I tell Aunt Sara
when the boys fall asleep
for the night.

Grace, stay out of trouble,
Aunt Sara warns.
*Your mama n Uncle Jim'll
be home soon.*

I promise, I say,
thinkin how happy
Mama will be
when she sees me.

In the light of the moon,
I run all the way to the swamp
where OleGeorgeCooper lives.

OleGeorgeCooper
used to be a slave
what worked in the fields
pickin cotton.
But one rainy night
he ran away.
He never got caught,
n now
he lives in the swamp
with gators, snakes,
n soul-stealin witches.

Sometimes, late at night,
OleGeorgeCooper
comes visitin.
Uncle Jim gives him
taters or squash
what's growin
in our garden.

OleGeorgeCooper's
got gray tears stuck
in the corner of his eyes,
n silver whiskers bloomin
through the ripple marks
what cross his face.

I used to be scared
of OleGeorgeCooper,
his stories,
his raspy voice,
his scratches.

The ripple marks
scared me most,
but Mama told me
they's jus scars.

Mama says scars
is nothin more'n
a body's memory.

Someday, Mama says,
the good Lord Himself'll
wash em away.
Mama says the man
what gave em—
what slashed n whipped,
what burned n branded—
one day,
that man's goin to tremble.

She smiles. *On that day,*
we'll see how beautiful
OleGeorgeCooper was
before meanness
got planted in the world.

Now I don't care nothin
bout the stories
OleGeorgeCooper tells.

I don't care bout gators
what's bigger n bumpier'n
sweet-gum bark.

I don't care bout the witch
what lives in the swamp,
what likes
to gobble children—
specially slave children.

I smear mud
deep into the skin
of my face,
arms, n legs.
My eyes sting,
but finally I'm brown.

Beautiful brown.

Brown like my mama
n my brothers,

brown like Uncle Jim
n Aunt Sara.
Brown like our great big family
what works in the fields.

When Mama sees me,
she drags me
to the wash barn
n dumps water on my head.
All my beautiful brown
disappears
in skinny little rivers
what look like tears.

Mama scrubs
till my skin's pale
as a brown bat's belly.
Why'd the good Lord
make my skin so light?
I cry.

Grace! Mama says.
This here's the skin
the good Lord gave you.
You's insultin the good Lord
to try n change it.

I'm only nine years old
but I'm old enough
to wonder why the good Lord
paints children different colors
from they mama,
makin em so they look stolen,
makin em feel
shamed of they own skin.

Dirt runs into my eye
n I holler.

Mama hushes me.
Grace, try to understand.
Master Allen say
he own us.
We got to do what he want
or somebody'll
get a whippin—
maybe even worse!

Don't seem fair, I say.

Mama's voice grows soft,
like when she's tellin
her nighttime stories bout
restin in the arms of angels.

The good Lord's sure weepin
at the way His children
is bein treated,
she says.
But for now,
there's nothin we can do.

My rightiness bubbles
inside me.

Don't the good Lord make
day n night?
I ask.
Don't the good Lord make
the giant trees
round the Big House?
Don't the good Lord make
thunder so loud
it shakes the earth?
I forget all bout
the pain in my eye.
Don't the good Lord have
more power'n Master Allen?

Mama spins me round so fast
I nearly fall in the mud.
You keep them thoughts
bound up tight
inside you, she says.
Or you'll be sent away—
far away—farther away'n
the Big House.

I promise, I say,
feelin prickles
scratch my throat.

That night Mama makes me
sit by my rag bed
n repeat all my promises.

You have to keep em,
she says,
cause the good Lord
n His angels is watchin—
if you break a promise,
they'll know
you can't be trusted.

Uncle Jim's workin outside
n I hear his deep voice
singin soft to the heavens.
Mama tells Thomas n Willy
I'm goin to the Big House
early-early in the mornin
before anyone wakes.
Says folks in the Big House
need someone
strong n brave n smart.

Willy toddles over to me
even though he's too young
to understand
what Mama said.
Thomas crawls after him.
I hug em both at the same time,
liftin em a little off the ground

n kissin they curls,
like I sometimes do,
makin soft, gibbery sounds
jus to hear em laugh.
Only this time
all my silly snuffles
get stuck inside my throat.

Aunt Sara puts down her mendin
n leads the boys
to they sleepin corner.
You's not goin far, Grace,
she whispers to me. *Be brave.*
Her eyes squint out a warnin.
Remember what I said.

Mama tears a narrow strip of cloth
from the hem of her dress
n kneels beside me.
She ties the frayed ribbon
round my bare ankle.
*May the good Lord n His angels
keep watch over my baby,*
she says.

Then she looks at me
with watery eyes.
My sweet Grace, she says,
you's tied to my heart forever.

I throw my arms round her
n make myself a promise
to never take off
her ribbon
n to keep
my mouth shut.

Early-early the next mornin
Uncle Jim walks with me
past the row of cabins
what's been my home forever,
n up the big hill
what's spotted with tiny flowers.

At the top of the hill,
we stop under a giant elm.
Uncle Jim stoops down.
His eyes set right cross
from my eyes,
n his hands curve
round my face.
Your mama told me the thoughts
runnin circles in your head, Grace.
They's dangerous thoughts—
you best keep em to yourself.

Mama already told me that, I say,
but soon as the words pop out, I'm sorry.

Uncle Jim's hands is
rough as tree bark,
but his voice is gentle
as the barn swallow.
I's meanin it, Gracie.
Keep em thoughts to yourself,
or you'll be bringin us all
a whole lot of trouble n pain.

Your mama's heart would break
if Master sent you away—
all our hearts would break.
He smooths my hair
n makes his voice real low.
Got to keep your thoughts
tucked private in your mind
where white folks won't find em.

Why? I got skin pale as any white folk—
I heared Mama say so herself.
It's my light skin
what got me called to the Big House.

Uncle Jim shakes his head.
Don't matter what color
the good Lord painted you,
he says, *you know that.*
Law says you's brown,
same as your mama.

The law's got a problem
seein what's right in front
of its face, I think,
but this time I say nothin,
n we keep walkin
to the Big House
what's on the other side
of the hill.

Aside of the Big House
is a covered walkway
with a cabin attached.

A woman older'n Mama,
but not as old as Aunt Sara,
n twice as wide,
stands waitin outside.

Uncle Jim nods at her.
Tempie, this here's our Grace.
Gracie, this is Aunt Tempie.

The woman smiles.
Hello, Grace.
Last time I saw you,
you was no bigger'n
a pitcher plant!
She looks at Uncle Jim.
Time passes.

That it does, Tempie.
Too quick—
or too slow.
I best get back.
He looks at me
with sorrowful eyes
n touches my face.
Remember what
we talked bout, Gracie.

I nod n will my tears
from fallin.
A heavy grievin
sags inside me,
n my thoughts leap
n tumble.

Uncle Jim n Mama
is jus down the hill.

If I got sent away,
I might never see
Mama or Aunt Sara,
Uncle Jim or the boys
ever again.

Mama was younger'n me
last time she saw her mama.

Come inside, Grace.
Aunt Tempie's voice is
deep n scratchy,
like she's got prickles
sittin in her throat too.
Still, it's a voice
with a kindness in it
what makes me feel safe.

We step into the cabin.

A huge fireplace
stretches from one corner
to another.
Sun's not even up yet
but a big black pot
hangs over a fire
what's lightin the room
n warmin it like midday.
Already a tray of biscuits
sits in a turtle-shaped hole
in the wall.

Aunt Tempie spreads her arms.
This here's our kitchen, Grace.
We mostly be workin in here.
In the middle of the room
is a big table what holds
a basket of strawberries
n a covered tub.

Giant spoons n buckets
hang from the ceilin
n there's a row of chairs
set gainst the wall.

Aunt Tempie sniffs
the biscuits
n nods for me to follow her
through a small door
what don't close all the way.

This room looks
like our cabin
cept it's smaller
n has a wooden floor.
In the corner
there's a small table
what's got a basket
n some sewin on it,
a chair, a footstool,
n a tiny fireplace
what don't look
big enough to warm a fly.

This is where we sleep,
Aunt Tempie says.

A gown hangs
on the back of the door,
n another smaller gown
is draped over the chair.
A bunch more baskets
is piled in the corner
n another gown is draped
cross a narrow wooden bed
what mus belong
to Aunt Tempie.

She pulls a pallet
from under the bed.
This is for you, she says.

The cabin gets even smaller,
n all my rightiness
shrinks
to a mournful sadness.

Aunt Tempie nods
at the gown
on the bed.
You's washed up real nice,
she says, *but the Missus*
wants you wearin a shirttail
what's never been near the field.
Go ahead now—get changed,
we got work to do.

I quick take off the gown
Mama made
n slip the new gown
over my head.

Mama was wrong.

The new gown scratches
same as the old.
It smells like chicken feathers
n fills my mouth
with a bitter taste
like molasses
what's been spoiled.

I follow Aunt Tempie
back into the kitchen.

She points to the basket
filled with strawberries.
You can slice the berries,
Grace, she says.
She shows me how
to wrap my fingers
round the knife handle,
cut out the green leaves,
n push the blade
through the berries.
Mind you, slice em thin,
n be careful
not to slice your fingers.

She lifts the cover
off the tub.
Inside is a mound
of chopped pork
flecked with green.
Aunt Tempie starts
rollin n squishin
small fists of meat
into little cakes.

There's a million questions
tumblin in my mind,
but my voice feels trapped

like a weevil in sap.
Lucky for me,
Aunt Tempie starts
talkin up a storm,
tellin me most everythin
I want to know.

*There's three others
what live in the Big House
n eat with us in the kitchen,*
she says.
*Uncle Moses, Anna, n Jordon.
Uncle Moses waits
on Master Allen—
helps him dress,
drives his wagon,
n tends the horses.
Anna waits on
the Missus—
helps her dress,
washes the clothes,
sweeps n dusts.
Jordon's only job is bringin
food from the kitchen
n servin Master Allen's table.*

Seems white folks in the Big House
can't do much for emselves.

Aunt Tempie lowers her voice.
You won't see much
of Master Allen—
she shakes her head—
but the Missus,
she comes in most every day.

Aunt Tempie stops rollin
n looks at me,
her eyes steady n serious.
The Missus is mean
as a hornet
what's protectin its nest.
Stay away from the Missus.

Hearin Aunt Tempie talk
bout the Missus,
n rememberin
what Aunt Sara said,
gives my legs n arms
prickly bumps
like when OleGeorgeCooper
first told me
bout the swamp witch.

When the kitchen door opens,
I jump.

Aunt Tempie laughs.
Nothin to be scared of, Grace.
Anna's still helpin the Missus
get out of her nightclothes.
This here is Jordon.
Jordon, meet Grace.
Grace'll be helpin me in the kitchen.

Jordon's skin's jus a shade
darker'n mine,
with lots of little dots
crossin his nose n cheeks,
n wavy hair the color
of the jewelweed
what grows in the swamp.

He tells me hello
but don't smile,
n I wonder
if he's missin his mama too.

Course, Jordon looks older'n me,
old enough to jump the broom—
old enough
to take care
of himself.

But I know he's missin someone.
Sometimes a folk's eyes say more'n
a folk's mouth.

Watch those fingers,
Aunt Tempie says,
n when I look down,
Jordon n her
move away from me
n start whisperin
like they's tellin
each other a secret.

I try to listen
but I'm too much
worryin bout my fingers.

When they turn
round again,
Aunt Tempie smiles,
n I wonder if she
was tellin Jordon
a secret bout me.

Pretty soon
the whole day
wakes up,
n Jordon starts arrangin
biscuits on a tray.
Aunt Tempie puts
hot sausage cakes
on another tray
what's got a cover so shiny
I can see my face.
The kitchen smells good—
jus breathin
makes my stomach cry.

I think of Mama n Uncle Jim,
already workin in the field,
suckin that sweet
tobacco smell
what makes a body
feel sick all over.

Mama n Uncle Jim
won't eat nothin
till the midday bell,
n even all day
won't eat near as much
as what Jordon's arrangin
for Master's breakfast.

Don't forget the syrup,
Aunt Tempie says,
n she gives Jordon
a pink glass pitcher
what's sittin
on its own silver tray.

I wonder why
Master n the Missus
get to eat right early
in the mornin
n folks what's been workin
got to wait till
the midday bell.

Don't seem fair,
but I remember
all my promises,
push away
my rightiness thoughts,
n wonder when
I get to eat.

After breakfast, the Missus
comes into the kitchen
wearin a circle dress
what bounces when she walks
n shows her pretty cloth shoes.

Before I put my eyes down,
I see her snarlin face
measurin the sugar
what's left in the tin.

The Missus's got dark hair
what's pulled back
n puffed on both sides.
Her eyes n nose pinch
together like she ate
too many wild berries
what grow near the swamp.

She's not mindin me at all,
but my mouth's dry
n my heart's poundin,
thinkin bout all my
warnins n promises.

I follow her cloth shoes
cross the wooden floor
n keep dryin

the same spoon.
A few more steps
n she'll be gone.

But at the door
her feet stop.

Grace, she snaps.

I'm too scared to look up.

*It shouldn't take all day
to dry a single spoon.
And remove that filthy,
disgustin
piece of cloth
from around your ankle.*

After we clean the kitchen,
me n Aunt Tempie go back
inside our cabin.
Aunt Tempie nods for me
to sit on her bed
n stoops to untie the ribbon
round my ankle.

My mama put it there.
The first words
I say all day
cling to my throat,
but I scrape em off
n let em fall
in jagged whispers.
She said a prayer
n told me
I was tied
to her heart forever.

Aunt Tempie lifts my chin.
Her hand smells
of oyster juice n lemon.
The Lord don't need a ribbon
to hear your mama's prayer,
she says,
n you don't need a ribbon
to remember your mama.

The things what we love,
we keep buried in our hearts.

Aunt Tempie pulls the pallet
from under her bed
n tucks Mama's ribbon
inside the seam
of the prickly wool blanket
what's sittin on top.

A baby'll always be
tied to her mama's heart,
she says real quiet,

n I wonder
how many babies
is buried
in Aunt Tempie's heart.

Finally we go outside.
Barely been one mornin,
but already seems like days
since Uncle Jim brought me here.

I wonder if Aunt Sara's
rollin the beds n sweepin.
I wonder if Willy's chasin Thomas.

I wonder if anyone's missin me.

. . . n that's the smokehouse,
n the dairy—
you'll be spendin lots of time there—
n that far buildin's the laundry.
Aunt Tempie points to a row
of giant kettles hangin from a log
what's restin on two large posts.
That's for the soap
n candle makin, she says.

She touches my cheek
with her rough, oyster fingers.
You'll get used to it here, Grace.
You won't lose the sadness—
folks what's made a slave
don't ever lose the sadness—
but you'll get used to it here.
Now let's get you a muffin
before we start preparin
Master's next meal.

I work all day
grindin corn into flour
n learnin how
to split a chicken
n pull away the bones.

Aunt Tempie tells me
how Jordon traveled
all the way
from one end of Virginia
to another,
by pretendin to be white.

Master Allen don't know it,
but Jordon's a runner.

She slaps a chicken breast
in a plate of flour.
He's got a wife n baby girl
he's never goin to see again—
not much Master Allen can do
to hurt him more'n that.

A shiverin sorrow
spreads through my bones.

No wonder
Jordon never smiles.

Aunt Tempie says
Master Allen n the Missus
have three meals a day—
four if you count
the tea n biscuits
the Missus makes Anna bring her
in the middle of the night.
Aunt Tempie says
we eat same
as folks in the field—
late in the mornin
when *early* chores is done
n again in the evenin
when *all* our chores is done.

A hole's growin
in my stomach,
part from hunger
n part from anger.

Shouldn't the folks
what work the hardest
eat more'n the folks
what don't work at all?

When we finish servin
Master n the Missus
a fine supper of chicken
smothered in cream,
when the kitchen's
scrubbed cleaner'n
mornin sunshine,
the Missus gives us
permission to eat.

Finally I meet Anna
n Uncle Moses.

Before she goes upstairs,
the Missus looks at Anna
with scrunched
n shrivelin eyes.
No lingerin, she says.

Anna's young n bony.
She sits at the table
with droopin shoulders
what make her look
like a scared rabbit
what's jus waitin
to scurry away.
Yes, ma'am, she says
in a sweet, silvery voice.

The Missus clomps away
in her cloth shoes,
n her circle dress swishes
the floor as she turns.

Anna smiles shyly.
She's got curls like mine,
but her skin's
a pretty copper color
what reminds me
of late-day sunshine.

I smile back,
wishin my skin
was as pretty
n coppery as Anna's.

Jordon sits with his back
straight as a wood plank
n eats real quiet.

Uncle Moses smiles,
but it's a sorrowin
kind of smile
what makes me think
of Mama.

Uncle Moses is thin
like Mama too,
only he's old—
old as Aunt Sara—
with wispy hair,
white n gray
as yesterday's ashes.
His voice is soft
n whispery.
Pleased to meet you, Grace,
he says.

Pleased to meet you too,
I say, wonderin
how he's strong enough
to tend the horses
when his voice is frail enough
to blow away.

Pleased to meet you too, Anna.

Again Anna smiles,
but suddenly,
before Aunt Tempie
even sits down,
Anna bolts up.
The Missus might need help
pullin back her bedsheets,
she says, noddin to me
as she hurries away.

I wonder what the Missus's
bedsheets is made of,
but more'n that,
I wonder
how everyone's fear
n sorrow
is already minglin
with mine.

Where does Anna sleep?
I ask Aunt Tempie
when all the dishes
is washed n put away,
when the wood's stacked
for mornin,
n I'm finally lyin
on my pallet.

On the floor
of the Missus's room.

What bout Jordon
n Uncle Moses?

They sleep in the attic.

How come Anna sleeps
in the Missus's room?

Aunt Tempie yawns
n her words
start drippin
slow as water
from a leakin bucket.
Cause sometimes
in the middle of the night,
the Missus needs
wet towels
to soothe way

her headaches.
Sometimes she needs
the chamber pot,
or if she can't sleep,
a drop from
the blue doctorin bottle
what Master Allen
keeps in the sideboard
next to his brandy.

What's a sideboard?
What's brandy? I ask,
but already Aunt Tempie's
breathin deep n heavy.

Grace, she says between snores,
mornin comes fast.
Save some questions
for tomorrow.

I close my eyes.
The pallet is hard as rock,
n I miss Mama,
but I'm glad I'm not sleepin
on the floor near the Missus.
I hold the hem of my blanket
n send Mama a message
through her angels.
Good night, Mama, I whisper.
I kept all my promises.

Aunt Tempie snores
even louder'n Uncle Jim,
but mornin does come quick.
Early-early, before the sun
even thinks of wakin,
we get up n start the fire.

Aunt Tempie sets water to boilin
for the taters
while I chop cold ham.
Even cold, the ham
smells so good,
it's hard not to pop a morsel
in my mouth.

Wait till we fry em,
Aunt Tempie says,
like she's readin
my thoughts.
*Ham patties taste
even better left over.*

At first light,
Jordon comes
to keep watch on things
while Aunt Tempie brings me
to the milkin barn.
She shows me how
to collect the cream
what rises to the top
of the milk pans.

Later today we'll churn,
she says.

The mornin horn blows
n I think of Mama
n Uncle Jim
n all the folks what's
jus goin to the fields.
I think of Aunt Sara
givin me a few more
minutes of sleep.
Long as you can,
hold on
to the sweet days
of childhood,
she'd say.

I think of Thomas n Willy
still dreamin
in beds of straw n rags.

I guess my sweet days
of childhood is over.

After breakfast,
the Missus comes
into the kitchen
wearin her circle dress
n cloth shoes.
I keep my eyes down
but feel her
standin over me.

Tempie, she says,
n her words
fall on my head
like rocks.
I noticed the ham
was cut every which way.
Be more careful—
irregular cuts
make the patties unpalatable.

The Missus takes the left over
patties what I can almost taste
n dumps em in the scrap heap.
I'll have Moses bring this batch
to the hogs, she says.

She leaves
without sayin a word to me,
but it feels like her fingers
is wrapped round my throat.

I'm sorry, I tell Aunt Tempie
when the Missus is gone.

Aunt Tempie shakes her head.
Nothin wrong with your choppin.
She's jus lettin you know
she's the one
what's got the power.

We clean the kitchen,
n Aunt Tempie takes me
back to the milkin barn.
She stands me on a stool,
n I push n pull the handle
till my shoulders ache.
Inside the barrel,
milk what's been
skimmed n sourin
begins to set.

Inside me,
surly thoughts
bout the Missus
do the same.

The next day Aunt Tempie
sends me to the milkin barn
by myself.

Master Allen n Moses is
crossin to the stable.
It's the first time I'm meetin
Master Allen,
n I feel a flutter of fear.
He's taller'n Uncle Moses,
with light hair
growin everywhere on his face
cept his chin,
n eyes what's bluer'n mine.

Moses nods to me.

I nod n quick put my eyes down.
It don't matter.
Master Allen jus keeps walkin
to the stable
like he don't even see me.

I open the heavy barn doors
n climb on the stool.
But before I pull the handle
once round,
I hear a whimperin
what sounds like a rabbit
bein killed by a fox.

Jumpin off the stool,
I open the door
n peek outside.

The man what watches over
slaves in the field
is leavin the smokehouse
with his whip.
When he crosses the hill,
I run to the smokehouse
n sneak inside.
Anna is wobblin to her feet,
her eyes gapin
when she sees me.
Grace! You best get out of here,
she cries, *or you'll get
a whippin too!*

He's gone, I say,
tryin hard
not to breathe in
the smoky smell
what makes me
feel like chokin,
n tryin even harder
not to look
at the hogs
what's danglin
from the ceilin.

Anna pushes me out the door.
You'll smell like smoke!
She'll know you was here!
Get out! Please!

But, Anna! What happened?

Anna limps beside me.
The Missus said I was lingerin.
I got to hurry back to the Big House.

Her wide eyes is glistenin
n her voice tremblin
like a rabbit what's been boxed.

Please be careful, Grace,
n don't tell nobody you saw me!

I go back to the milkin barn,
climb the stool, n start churnin.

With every push n pull,
I try hard to heave away
the angry, hateful words
I promised Mama
I wouldn't say.

Every day I learn
somethin new.
I learn how to peel, chop,
mix, grind,
n bend my legs
so my arms
is strong enough to lift
the iron pots
what hang over the fire.
I skim, churn,
n lower left over butter
into the butter well
to keep cool.

At night when I sleep,
my legs feel like they's
still bendin,
my fingers feel like they's
still choppin,
n my arms feel like they's
still churnin.

My body feels weak
as a wet rag what can't stand
less someone's holdin it.

There's no ghosty sounds
in Aunt Tempie's room,

but my wool blanket's coarse
n prickly as straw.

I lie awake
pinchin n scratchin.
I hold the hem
what hides
Mama's ribbon
n listen to
Aunt Tempie snore.

I think bout Anna—
sweet as honey—
what does everythin
the Missus asks,
but still gets a whippin.

I think bout the Missus
n her sour face
what's always
snarlin n quiverin.

But mostly
I think bout Mama,
n try figurin a way
to see her.

Absolutely not,
Aunt Tempie clucks
when I present my plan.

But, Aunt Tempie, I say,
no one will ever find out—
I won't leave
till after Anna brings the Missus
her evenin tea,
n I'll be back here early-early
before the sun even thinks of risin.
I promise, Aunt Tempie! I promise!

No! Aunt Tempie says,
n don't be gettin any ideas
bout sneakin out
when I'm sleepin—
if the Missus don't catch you
n send you to the smokehouse,
I'll take you there myself.

I know Aunt Tempie's jus huffin,
but scaredness
creeps up my spine
jus the same.

Ever since I heared her
whimperin,
Anna n me
been stealin glances
n sneakin words.
The Missus keeps Anna
too busy
for us to talk long,
but there's always time
for a quick smile.
Mama says a smile
can lift a heart
what's heavier'n stone.

I think bout Mama
all the time
n beg Aunt Tempie
most every day
to let me visit her.

Finally one Saturday,
when I been livin
at the Big House
near a month,
Aunt Tempie tells me
she got a surprise.
But it's a secret
n before I tell you,
you got to make me
a promise.

Mama says
if you make a promise,
you should keep it
cause the good Lord's
always listenin.
If you break a promise,
the good Lord n His angels'll know
you can't be trusted,
she says.

I wonder if they stop
watchin over you too.

Can you promise?

I promise.

Don't seem like the good Lord's
payin me much mind anyway.
Every mornin I wake up,
I wake up here.

Aunt Tempie smiles.
I think it'll be safe
to visit your mama
while I help Anna
with the laundry.
Be back before sunup,
n no runnin—
there's roots n brambles
all round—
if you fall,
n the Missus finds out
you was outside at night,
we'll both get a whippin.

Sweet joy
bubbles inside me.

I promise promise promise!

Outside is dark n quiet,
but stars sparkle n shimmer
bright as angel wings.
It's hard to keep my feet
from runnin
n my breath
from liftin me away,
but I don't want the Missus
to find out
so I walk slow n careful.

When I reach the giant elm,
I stop to thank the good Lord
for listenin to my prayers,
even when I thought
He wasn't mindin me at all.

From the elm,
dependin on how
I turn my head,
I can see
the Big House or
Mama's cabin.

I turn n see Aunt Tempie's
large, loomin shadow
leavin the Big House,
carryin a small load
what mus be laundry,
only she's walkin

away from the wash barn
n into the dark.

Where's she goin?

I turn to Mama's cabin
n feel a tug in my heart,
rememberin
what Uncle Jim told me,
bout how Mama's heart
would break
if I got sent away,
n how I had to keep
my thoughts
tucked private in my mind.

For weeks,
my mind's been
so crowded with thoughts,
I'm afraid
they's goin to spill.

Finally my feet take me
to our cabin.
It's so late, even Uncle Jim
mus be inside,
givin his tired body a rest.

I'm worried I might scare em—
paddyrollers what come
lookin for runaways
come late at night too.

I never seen a paddyroller,
but I heared all bout em.
They's meaner'n
the Missus.
Paddyrollers go out at night
with whips n pistols,
lookin for runaways.
If they find em,
they tie em to a post
n thrash em
till they bleed.
Paddyrollers
what don't find trouble
make it emselves.
Even if a folk's jus sittin
in they cabin prayin,
or learnin emselves letters,
paddyrollers'll
pull em outside n whip em.

Most travel in packs
like wild dogs,
but I heared OleGeorgeCooper
say he's seen sneaky ones
what break from the pack
to make they own trouble.

I open the door slow—
so not to scare anyone—
but Mama's right there
on the other side of the door,
like she was jus waitin.

Did one of her angels
whisper I was comin?

She wraps her arms round me
n kisses my face
like we kiss Thomas n Willy—
givin em hundreds of kisses at once
jus to hear em laugh.

Then she starts cryin,
her wet face smilin.
I's so happy to see you!

I'm happy too, but I don't cry
cause there is nothin
but sweet joy inside me.

Aunt Sara n the boys
stir but don't wake up.
Mama pushes me away,
but only to take a better look.
You growed so big, she says,
n Uncle Jim whisper-laughs.
Catherine! It's barely been a month.

But I know how Mama feels.
When you love someone so much
n you been with em forever,
a day away feels like a year.

Mama looks different too.
Her face is still skinny
but there's squishy puffs
round her eyes
like beans what's been
soakin in broth.

I miss you too, Mama, I say,
but my words
is so much smaller'n
the feelin inside me.

I leave for the Big House
early-early,
when black shrivels
into purple,
long before the white folks
wake up.

The kitchen fire's already blazin
n Jordon n Aunt Tempie
is talkin quietly.
Jordon nods a good mornin
when I come in,
but Aunt Tempie jus points
to the taters what need peelin.

On Sundays,
Master n the Missus
eat breakfast before
they leave for church.
They need to keep up they strength
for the pastor's sermon,
Aunt Tempie told me
first Sunday I was here.

Don't know why
folks need strength
to do nothin but sit n listen.
Aunt Tempie jus tells me
to do what I'm told
n not ask so many questions.

Folks what work in the fields
don't eat nothin
till the midday bell,
I argue anyway,
but Aunt Tempie don't care.
She don't even ask
bout my visit with Mama.

After breakfast,
the Missus comes
into the kitchen
wearin her Sunday best.
Pig should have been
roastin by now,
she says.
You know how hungry
Master Allen gets
after a long mornin in church.

I feel the Missus's eyes
watchin me
n wonder if she knows
I sneaked out
to visit Mama.

After my first visit,
Aunt Tempie lets me
visit Mama
every Saturday, late-late,
when Master n the Missus
is sleepin.
Sometimes Aunt Tempie
lets me take left over
muffins n cakes
what's startin to get stale.

Every time she sees me,
Mama shakes her head
n tells me it's the last time,
that if Master Allen
ever finds out,
he'll send me far away.

Then she wraps me
in her arms.
She whispers
how she misses me,
how she loves me
more'n flowers
love sunshine.
Sometimes Thomas n Willy
wake up n curl round my legs
like worms on a tobacco leaf.

I'm always back early-early
so Aunt Tempie
won't change her mind
bout lettin me go.

I don't see Mama
till the followin Saturday,
but I carry her whispers
in my heart
all week.

Cept for churnin days,
I stay in the kitchen
helpin Aunt Tempie.

I peel taters into a bucket,
n scrape all the brown
off the carrots.

We work quiet cause
the Missus
don't like noise
n gets headaches
most every day.

If Aunt Tempie
burns the bread
n sputters too loud,
or I squeal at a weevil
what's burrowed
in a carrot,
we hear the Missus
bustle through the walkway
into the kitchen.

*Perhaps you'd do better
farther south,*
she says to Aunt Tempie.
*Perhaps a whippin
will make you braver,*
she says to me.

How does whippin
make a body brave?
I wonder,
but I clamp
my mouth shut
so no words
escape.

My favorite day is Sunday,
even though there's more work
cause dinner's earlier
n Master stays home
flectin on what
the preacher tells him
is holy thoughts,
n the Missus wants us
lookin extra busy.

But I don't mind
cause when Master's thinkin
his holy church thoughts,
I'm flectin on my visit
with Mama.

One Sunday mornin,
before they leave for church,
the Missus comes into
the kitchen
directin Aunt Tempie
bout some spot
on a silver spoon.
I'm openin a yellow squash
n rememberin
Willy's sweet smile
when I gave him
my muffin surprise.
Now they don't see me
so much, Mama don't

shush em back to sleep
if they wake up
when I visit.

I'm jus bout to scoop out
the insides of the squash
when a pale green worm
big as my thumb
uncurls its restin body,
n I squeak.

The Missus walks over.
Afraid of a worm?
she asks.

No, ma'am. Jus startled.

*Well, perhaps that whippin
we talked about
will make you braver,*
she says,
turnin to leave.

Whippin don't make you brave,
I think, but this time—
without any warnin—
my thoughts spill
into sound.
I cover my mouth n hope
the Missus don't hear,

but she turns right round
in those pretty cloth shoes
n looks at me
with red-hot flames
flickerin
in her eyes.

Before I can look down,
her fingers flash
cross my cheek
like broom whiskers
what's on fire.

Put those haughty eyes down,
she says.
If I weren't goin to church,
I'd send you for a whippin.

I put my eyes down
n hold back the tears
what burn almost as much
as the Missus's fingers
what crossed my face.

Aunt Tempie brings me
a new squash
but don't say nothin till we hear
Master Allen n the Missus
leave for church.

Grace, she finally says,
I know your daddy told you—

He's not my daddy,
I say,
tears spillin
from my eyes.

Aunt Tempie wipes em away
with her apron.
But he loves you
like a daddy,
she says quietly,
n that's what matters.
Things is goin to change, Grace.
The good Lor—

The good Lord
don't care bout us,
I say.

Aunt Tempie shakes her head.
You can't blame
the good Lord
for what people do.

Thinkin like that'll make
a mind crazy.
Things'll change, Grace,
maybe even sooner'n later,
but till they do—

Things won't change
less we change em,
I say,
angry at Aunt Tempie
for jus ceptin things
the way they is.

It's not fair,
I say,
n all the thoughts
what's been pilin
in my head tumble out.
Why can't she polish
her own silver?
Why can't she bake
her own muffins?
Why do grown folks
need help gettin dressed?

I finish scoopin squash
n turn my eyes
from the ragged chicken
Aunt Tempie keeps dippin
in the pot.

Even Thomas n Willy
dress emselves,
n they's jus toddlers.
Willy's only had but
two birthdays,
n Thomas is even younger.

Aunt Tempie plucks a feather,
nods to herself,
n pulls the chicken from the pot.
I know she's listenin to me,
but she keeps her mouth closed
n lets me babble.
Jus talkin bout Thomas n Willy
makes me miss em even more.
Feels like they's right
in the kitchen with me,
n not jus some ghosty thoughts
what ramble in my mind.

Sometimes Willy walks round
with his gown stuck on his head,
wobblin n bumpin into things,
but that's jus pretend.
That's jus Willy bein silly
to make folks laugh.
Willy knows how
to dress himself
sure as the sun
knows how to shine.

Aunt Tempie goes right on
pattin the chicken dry
without sayin a word to me.

Don't you care? I ask.
*Don't you care that Anna
gets sent to the smokehouse
cause grown people
can't find they own bedpan
or even dress emselves?*

*The only dressin
we need to worry bout
is this here chicken,*
Aunt Tempie says.
Start pluckin.

My blood boils hotter'n
burnt puddin,
but Aunt Tempie jus
starts choppin oysters
n hummin soft
to herself.

I won't even look at her.
How can she not care?

The Missus comes back
from church
n takes to her bed
cause Master's brother
n his new wife, Charlotte,
is comin for a late supper.

I hear her tellin Anna,
Rest makes a body strong,
n I feel like chokin.

Slaves hardly ever rest
n we's stronger'n
Master Allen
n the Missus
put together.

While we polish the silver,
Aunt Tempie tells me
whenever guests visit,
Master Allen asks Jordon
to serve
with his eyes blindfolded.

I'm still mad
so I pretend
I don't hear
Aunt Tempie talkin.

Aunt Tempie pretends
she don't notice me
ignorin her.
*Master Allen ties a white rag
round Jordon's eyes,*
she says.

The silver's bright enough
to chase the stars away,
but I pretend
there's a tarnish spot
what's takin all my
concentratin.

That evenin,
Aunt Tempie lets me
peek through the keyhole.

Jordon, show my brother
and his wife
how well you serve,
Master Allen says.

Jordon places the plates
in all the right places
without knockin anythin over.
Then he steps back.

Master Allen laughs.
What about our water?

I worry what might happen,
but Jordon turns to the table
behind him,
reaches for the silver pitcher,
n pours water in every glass.
He don't spill a drop.

The Missus claps,
n Master's brother laughs,
but his wife jus looks down.

Master Allen starts eatin
with his chest puffed out
like an overstuffed pastry.

You may remove
the blindfold, Jordon,
he finally says.

Jordon steps back again
n unties the blindfold.

His face is set
like stone
n his eyes
empty as glass.

I wonder what thoughts
is runnin
through his mind,

but seems even
without a blindfold,
Jordon's wearin
a mask.

Later that night,
Jordon's still standin
by the side table
waitin on Master Allen
n his brother
while they's smokin pipes
n drinkin brandy.
Uncle Moses, Aunt Tempie,
Anna, n me
is eatin left over dumplins
n worryin bout Jordon.

The Missus comes
into the kitchen
with Miss Charlotte
n starts showin off
the turtle-shaped warmin oven
what's built into the wall.
Anna jumps up,
n the pitcher
what's sittin
in the middle
of the table
tips over.
Cider seeps
through the cracks
n onto the floor.

Clean it up, Anna,
the Missus says sweetly.
We'll deal with this
when our guests leave.

Anna's wide,
frightened eyes
break open
the tinderbox
what's keepin
my dangerous thoughts
bound up tight
inside me.

In the smokehouse?
I whisper.

Soon as
my words
escape,
I'm sorry.

The Missus shoots me
an evil, threatenin snarl
what makes
all my rightiness
wither to ash.
I'm tremblin inside,
but before the Missus
can say anythin,
Miss Charlotte
asks me my name.

Grace, I choke out.

Grace. What a lovely name,
Miss Charlotte says.
And what pretty eyes you have.
She turns to Anna.
Accidents happen—
why just yesterday
I spilled cream all over
my new tablecloth.
The Missus can't
do nothin but smile
when Miss Charlotte adds,
What lovely helpers
you have, Gertrude.

The Missus n Charlotte leave,
n Anna n Moses

follow after em.
I'm already feelin
like a pile
of tobacco worms
is hatchin
in my stomach
when I hear
the Missus interrupt
Miss Charlotte's
sweet chatterin.

Oh! Excuse me, Charlotte,
I forgot to remind Tempie
about your husband's fondness
for blackberries,
the Missus says
in a high, sweet,
silvery voice
I never heared
her use before.
Anna, show Miss Charlotte
into the parlor.
I'll be with you
in a moment.

I hear the shuffle
of the Missus's cloth shoes
n the swish of her circle dress
turnin in the walkway.

Aunt Tempie looks at me
with knowin eyes
what signal me
to keep mine down.

The Missus comes
into the kitchen
n stands so close to me,
I smell her oyster breath.
She takes the dish I'm clearin
n gives it to Aunt Tempie.
Ghosty cold fingers brush
my shakin hands,
n I stare at the floor.

That's right, she hisses.
You keep those eyes down.
Perhaps you think
your pale skin
gives you the right
to speak your mind.
But, my dear haughty child,
you are nothin but a slave
who needs to learn her place.

A smile dances
between her words.
And since you are so interested
in the smokehouse,
I'll be sure to send you there
when my guests leave.

She turns to Aunt Tempie
n with her strange
new silvery voice says,
Tempie, add
blackberry cobbler
n fresh cream
to the breakfast menu.
I'm sure Grace won't mind
gatherin berries in the dark.
I don't believe bears
will be foragin this late.

A chillin fear
wraps round my bones
n chokes my breath.

I don't look up
till I hear
the Missus's cloth shoes
clomp into the hallway.

Jordon finally comes inside,
n I can tell by his pitiful look
he was listenin at the door.

Nothin but misery in a corset,
Aunt Tempie whispers.

Come with me, Grace,
Jordon says.
*There's some blackberry bushes
just beyond the stable.*
He looks at Aunt Tempie.
I'll eat when I get back.

Aunt Tempie nods
n gives me a basket.
*I'll take care of the cleanup.
Half a basket's all I need.
Don't press the berries down.*

I take the basket
n follow Jordon out the door.
My whole body's shakin,
n a cold dread
chokes
my rightiness voice
silent.

It's dark outside,
n the sky's got
a ripple
of white clouds
what's coverin the stars.
Each step away
from the house yard
my breathin gets easier,
but my words
is still witherin
like smoke.

Jordon's quiet too.
The only sounds is
the rustle of our feet
n the shrilly chirps
of lonesome
crickets n tree frogs
callin for mates.

I once heared
OleGeorgeCooper
tell Uncle Jim
that fear's got a way
of creepin inside
a grown man,
stealin his voice,
n stranglin
his soul.

Fear's got my voice,
but for Mama's sake,
I'm tryin hard
to hold on to
my soul.

The sky bove the stable
is clear of clouds,
n the moon casts
a dusty light.

A line of scraggily bushes
lean gainst the stable wall.

Jordon stomps the ground.
Don't think we'll see a bear,
but maybe a rattler, he says.

He waits a moment,
jus listenin,
then reaches deep
into the middle branches.
Lots of thorns, he says,
but lots of berries too.
You hold the basket—
this won't take long.

When the basket's bout
half full, he stops.
Now you reach in and take a few.
The thorns will scratch,
but if the Missus doesn't see
scrapes on your hands,
she'll wonder why.

What bout the scratches
on your hands? I ask.

When the Missus sees em,
she'll know you helped me.

Hidden by the white gloves
they make me wear,
Jordon says, almost smilin.
You've got to beat em
at their own game.

Thanks for helpin me,
I say in a whispery voice
what don't even sound
like mine.

Jordon nods.
I've got my own baby girl,
younger than you.
I hope if she's ever in trouble
someone'll be there
to help her.

Jordon's voice is low n sad.

I hope so too, I whisper,
n a little of my fear
melts into sorrow.

The next day, the Missus
comes into the kitchen
early-early.
The ghosty dread
what's been followin me
everywhere
keeps me from lookin up.
Tempie, is that
blackberry cobbler?
It smells divine.

The Missus walks
round the kitchen
sniffin n snoopin
till she's standin
right over me.
Good mornin, Grace,
she says cheerfully.
I trust there were no bears
in the blackberry patch—
but, oh dear,
look at those scratches!

I clamp my mouth shut.

They do look like they hurt—
though certainly
not as much as a whippin.

The Missus takes the salt jar
what's sittin on the table,
sprinkles my hands, n smiles.

I believe salt
prevents infections.
Go ahead, Grace,
rub in the salt.

I rub the salt,
gentle as I can,
while the Missus watches.

Well, I best get back
to my guests.
She looks at Aunt Tempie.
I cannot wait to taste
that cobbler.

My hand burns n stings,
but still I'm happy—
I didn't let
a single cry
escape.

The scratches
on my hands
make everythin
more painful,
n I wonder if
Jordon's sufferin too.

He's got wounds
much worse'n
blackberry scratches,
Aunt Tempie says.
Maybe now you'll learn
to keep your mouth closed.

Aunt Tempie's words
start my huffiness
simmerin again.
How come
she don't care?

She even sends me back
to the blackberry bushes.
Best to keep
Master happy,
she says,
stirrin sugar n
fresh blackberries
into boilin water.
Goin to send
his brother home

with a jar of our best
blackberry syrup.

Aunt Tempie knows
the Missus is mean.
She knows Master Allen
don't care bout us.
Why does she care
bout makin him happy?

Even if fear
steals my soul,
I'm never goin to coddle
grown people
what's got
no sense
of kindness.

The next day,
when Miss Charlotte
n her husband
finally leave,
the Missus gets
one of her headaches.

Your mama mus be
prayin for you!
Aunt Tempie says.
Thought for sure
you'd be goin
to the smokehouse.

I thought so too
n wonder why
the good Lord listens
to some prayers
n not others.

Still,
there's a tremblin
inside me
what'll never go away
long as I'm livin
at the Big House.

Ever since Jordon walked with me
to the blackberry bush,
I been thinkin bout his little girl
n wonderin what she looks like.
I wonder if she's got
pale skin like Jordon
n if she'll pretend to be
white like he did.

When my arms ache
from turnin sour milk to butter,
I wonder what it's like
to do nothin
but sit on soft chairs—
to wait n be served
muffins or taters smothered
in the fresh butter
someone else churned.

One night, before we go to bed,
I ask Aunt Tempie
if she thinks I could pass
for white.
My skin's even lighter'n Jordon's.

You sure could,
Aunt Tempie says.
*But you best not get any ideas
in that pretty little head of yours.
Passin for white's as dangerous
as followin the star.*

I don't know what
followin the star means,
so Aunt Tempie
takes me outside.
She points to the dark sky.
See them stars
what look like my soup ladle?
she whispers.
They's pointin north.
They's pointin to Freedom.
Aunt Tempie puts her arms
on my shoulders.
There's a whole beautiful
world out there, Grace—
the good Lord made it
for everybody.

Then why, I wonder,
do you work so hard
jus to please Master Allen?
Why does Jordon
have a baby girl
he's never goin to see again?

But I keep these thoughts
tucked private in my mind.

We go back inside
n climb into our beds.
Soon as Aunt Tempie
lays herself down,
she's deep asleep n snorin.
I lay awake a long time
thinkin bout the place
called Freedom.

I figure it mus be
somewhere near heaven.
Mama says heaven's
behind the clouds,
n it looks to me
like the ladle stars point
in the same direction.

Don't know much
bout Freedom,
but I do know a lot
bout heaven.

In heaven,
Mama says,
the good Lord loves everybody,
no matter what color
they's painted.
In heaven, the good Lord
won't allow nobody
to take a mama's child,

or threaten to whip her
cause she don't like weevils
hidin in the carrots,
or she accidently
spills cider
on the kitchen floor.

In heaven
Jordon's baby girl'll be sittin
on his shoulders,
reachin for the moon.

Seems Freedom mus be
right round the corner
from heaven.

I fall asleep jumpin
from star to star,
pretendin I'm on my way
to Freedom,
n hopin
I wake up there.

On Saturday night
Mama asks me
bout the scratches
on my hand,
n I tell her bout
the delicious
blackberry cobbler
Aunt Tempie made.
Worth every scratch, I lie.

Mama looks like
she don't believe me,
so I hurry n tell her bout
the blackberry jam.
*Only now I know
not to eat too much,*
I say.

Mama laughs,
both of us rememberin
when I first discovered
the wild berries
what grow near the swamp.
I ate so many,
my belly hurt for days.

I miss my girl,
Mama says,
but I's happy you's workin

in the Big House
n gettin to eat good food.
She snuggles closer.
I was worried bout
how the Missus would treat you.
She's always been a mean one.

Through the open window,
soft moonlight
casts a white shadow
on Mama's sorrowin face.

I don't like lyin
to Mama—
but tellin her
the truth
would be worse.

Seems I'm jus fallin asleep
when Mama shakes me awake.
Almost daylight, sweet baby.
Time to go back.

She opens the cabin door
to watch me leave like always.

Like always
she makes me promise
to mind the Missus
n don't talk back.

Like always
I hold her tight
n promise—

only this time,
I know my promisin's a lie
cause I already broke it.

Mama's holdin me tight
but a shameful sadness
squeezes between us.

Outside, the stars
is still danglin
in the purple
darkness—
not a trail
of ladle stars,
but loose stars,
runaway stars,
stars too stubborn
to disappear.

Shame n sadness
cling
to my heart
as I climb the hill
n wonder
if some poor slave's
countin on
a loose star's
fearless light.

Is some poor slave
followin its
defiant gleam
all the way to Freedom?

What if that slave
was me?

Only way to shake
my shame is by
makin myself
a new promise
to mind all the rules.

If I see a weevil
hidin in a carrot,
or a worm
nappin in a sweet tater,
I'll flick it away
without makin a peep.

If the Missus
is cross
or havin one of her
headaches,
I'll keep my eyes down
n let her words
thrash me
without once
lookin up
or makin a sound.

It's almost harvesttime
n Aunt Tempie's
been givin me
extra warnins.
Master Allen'll be frettin

n the Missus'll be fussin,
she says.

Seems harvesttime's
the perfect time
to start a new promise.

I won't ever try to please
Master Allen n the Missus
like Aunt Tempie does,
but I'll make Mama happy
by helpin best I can
n stayin out of trouble,
specially at harvesttime.

On the first day of the harvest
heavy rains pound the roof
n slosh in the yard.
Master Allen is up early.

*Harvestin wet'll
make a body sick,*
Aunt Tempie says,
grindin ginger
n throwin it into a pot
of boilin water.
*Master Allen'll be
worried bout
his tender tobacco
gettin moldy—*

*soon enough he'll be
comin in here
lookin for somethin
to keep a body
workin the field
even if they's sick.*

We hear Master Allen's footsteps
in the walkway,
n Aunt Tempie looks at me
with her knowin eyes.

Tempie, Master Allen says,
not noticin me at all,
you need to grin—

The Missus comes in
lookin like she's seen
the swamp witch.

We've more problems
than wet tobacco
and sick field hands,
she says,
her voice sputterin
like fat on a fire.
Jordon has run away.

Master Allen's
sharp blue eyes flash
n he hurries out.
The Missus follows
behind him
but Aunt Tempie
tells me
to keep peelin
n mashin.

They's still goin to eat,
she says.

Did Jordon really run away?
I ask, worryin bout
the whippin he'll get
when Master Allen finds him.

Rain's best time for runnin—
dogs can't catch your scent,
Aunt Tempie whispers.
Works better'n pepperin
your tracks.

My stomach's flutterin
with worries bout Jordon,
but Aunt Tempie
goes right on grindin
knots of ginger.
All those secrets she shares
with Jordon n still
she don't care bout nothin
but pleasin Master Allen.

Where is her heart?

I don't stop mashin
but I thank the good Lord
for sendin rain
n pray He remembered
to leave a star
lingerin somewhere
in the swampy sky.

Uncle Moses brings
Master Allen
his fritters,
n Anna serves the Missus.

It's still rainin midday,
n my worries
n wonderins
bounce back n forth
from Jordon
to Mama
to Uncle Jim
n all the folks
what's workin in the fields,
breathin the revoltin smell
of wet tobacco.

Aunt Tempie's showin me
how to cut a hog for picklin—
feet in one pot,
ears n nose in another—
when the Missus
comes into the kitchen.

As you know, she says,
her eyes dartin round
the room like Jordon's
hidin in the pots,
n scowlin at me
like I put him there,

Jordon has run away.
I've no doubt
he will be back,
but until he returns,
we will get by
in the dinin room
with a shift of duties.

Her eyes fix on me
n dance a little.
A ghosty cold
shivers up my spine.

Grace, you will take
Jordon's place.
She looks at Aunt Tempie.
Grace has been
coddled long enough.
She's old enough
to do real work.
She looks at me
like she's smellin stinkybugs.
Mind you,
Jordon's white gloves won't fit,
so clean under those nails
before you touch
my dinner plates.

That afternoon,
Aunt Tempie
scrubs my hands
with a corncob,
but no matter how hard
she brushes,
my fingers don't seem
clean enough.

Why can't they get
they own food?
I ask,
even though I already know.
White folks in the Big House
won't be happy
less they have people like me
to boss round.

Aunt Tempie ignores me
n goes on scrubbin n inspectin.

They can't cook or clean
or even dress emselves—
n they's not strong enough
to work in the fields,
or even carry a plate of crab cakes
to the table.
Cept for Miss Charlotte,
they's all mean as cottonmouths
n not as smart.

Aunt Tempie hushes me.
Can't be thinkin that way,
she says.
Or you is jus as bad as them.
Judgin folks by the color
of they skin is wrong—
no matter who's
doin the judgin.

She turns my hands over.
You stand tall n don't let
the Missus see you shakin,
she says,
n one more thing.
Master Allen likes to think
he's the only one
with thoughts behind his eyes,
so don't be showin him
you understand more'n
what he tells you.

It's not fair, I say,
worryin how long
I can keep my thoughts
from spillin again.

Aunt Tempie dries my hands
with her apron.
Grace, there's plenty
of white folks
like Miss Charlotte,

plenty of white folks
what's kind, what know
keepin slaves is wrong.
Jordon says there's
a white folk what
helped hide him.
Says up north
there's even a few
what's workin
to get laws changed.

She takes a deep breath
n lets it out slow.
Times is changin, Grace.
Jordon says soon
the whole world's
goin to wake up.
Soon the whole world's
goin to see
we all got the same blood
runnin rivers inside us.

Thinkin of Jordon
makes us both quiet.
Aunt Tempie turns my hands over
to inspect em one more time.
You jus got to pray
that soon comes soon,
she finally says.

For the rest of the day
I try to pray for Jordon
n the folks
workin in the field,
but I jus keep worryin
bout myself.
By dinnertime
my legs n arms
is shakin.

Stand tall, Aunt Tempie says,
handin me the soup tureen.

I take a deep breath,
n straighten my back
like I seen Jordon do.
I walk right into
the dinin room
n place the barley soup
in the middle of the table.
Real careful I lift the lid
n place it upside down
on the sideboard,
like Aunt Tempie showed me.

The whole time,
the Missus is watchin,
waitin for me to make a spill.

Real slow I dip the fancy white ladle
into the thick brown soup.

I pour a single scoop
into each empty bowl.

Grace! Be careful!
the Missus says.
These dishes come
all the way
from England.
They are irreplaceable!

Yes, ma'am, I say,
n hope the Missus don't see
my hand quiverin
like a cat's tail.

When I'm done pourin,
I step back.

I stand straight n tall,
like a ribbon's
pullin my neck to the ceilin.

I stare straight ahead
without blinkin,
like my eyelids
is stitched to my brows.

Still as a block of stone
I stand, but inside me,
thoughts crash n clatter.

Outside my chatterin mind,
the only sounds
is the scratch
of silver spoons
scrapin the fancy bowls
what come all the way
from England.
Master Allen
don't say a word.
Neither do the Missus.
Aunt Tempie's barley soup
smells so good,
my stomach starts grumblin
real loud,
but Master Allen n the Missus
is too busy scrapin,
too busy sippin n soppin
to hear my empty stomach.

Bring out the next course, Grace,
Master Allen finally says.

I start into the kitchen,
but the Missus stops me.
Grace! Clear away the tureen
and these used dishes!
Civilized people
keep a civilized table!

Fear shimmies up my spine.
But then I hear a voice—
not a speakin voice,
but a voice inside me—

They's no better'n you,
the voice says,
n I think Mama
mus be callin on
the good Lord
to watch over me.

A courage comes on me,
like angel wings
is liftin me up
n carryin me,
shivers n all.

After Master Allen
is stuffed
with beef n taters,
he sits back in his chair
n starts talkin to the Missus
like I'm not there.

I'll wait another day.
He'll come back.
He'll be tired, wet,
and hungry.
He'll come back.

He might have friends
to help him get away,
the Missus says.
Perhaps an advertisement
placed in a
more timely manner
would be prudent.

Master Allen looks up.
His eyes cut the air
like shards of blue glass.

I said I'll wait another day!

The Missus stands up.
Grace! she snaps.
Ask Anna what happens

to slaves who slouch.
She puts her hand
to her head.
I believe Anna
is in the kitchen.
Tell her to come upstairs
immediately.
I feel a headache
comin on.

I do as the Missus says
without sayin a word,
but I wonder
if her head only aches
so she can ballyrag Anna.

The next Saturday
Aunt Tempie won't let me
visit Mama.

But I visit Mama
every Saturday!
If Mama don't see me
she'll worry—
she'll be cryin herself
to sleep, for sure,
I argue.

We'll get word to her,
Aunt Tempie says.
Things is different now.
You got to be here
if the Missus
comes lookin for you.

Worryin bout Mama
feels like worms
is crawlin in my belly.
I'm so mad at Aunt Tempie,
I squint my eyes till I feel
wrinkles in my forehead.

But Aunt Tempie don't care.
Good night, Grace, she says.

I pretend I'm already asleep.

When I hear her snorin
like a bee in clover,
I get up.
I slip on my day gown
n tiptoe into the kitchen.

I'm jus bout to step
outside
when I hear a
clatter n bump
from inside
the Big House.

I creep into the walkway
n peek through the keyhole.

Anna is on her knees
pickin up the pieces
of a broken bowl
what come all
the way from England.

I open the door quietly—
n when she looks up
I see great big tears
runnin down
her face.

Don't cry, Anna, I say.
I'll help you clean up.

She's goin to send me
to the smokehouse
for sure, Grace.
Then she's goin to
send me away.
Says next time
I bump
or spill somethin,
she's goin to send me south.
Told Master Allen
I'm not worth

an empty cask
what's got bugs in it.

That's not true, Anna,
I say.
Bring the candle closer.
If we pick up
all the shatterins,
maybe she won't notice.

The Missus notices
everythin, Anna says.

Why you down here,
anyway? I ask.

The Missus is feelin queasy.
Came to get her medicine
n she says she wants you
to bring her some mint tea.

Me?

Anna nods.
I heard her tell Master Allen
she brought you here
to take my place.
She's goin to sell me, Grace.
She says slaves

what's got pale skin
is smarter'n slaves
what look like me.
Master Allen agrees
you is a good vestment
n said they should've
brought you up sooner.

What's a vestment?
I ask,
but Anna shrugs.

Anyway, I say, *jus cause a folk*
says somethin
don't make it true.
Skin's got nothin to do
with smartness.
We both got jus as many
smart thoughts
as Master Allen—
only we got to keep em
bound up
inside us.

Anna looks up.
Her face is dry,
but her eyes
still brim.

Grace!
Aunt Tempie is standin
in the doorway.
She whispers my name,
but it slices the air
sharp as a butcherin knife.

I jus came to get her,
Anna says.
The Missus wants Grace
to bring her some tea.

Aunt Tempie
looks at me
like the Missus do,
with squinty eyes
n a scowlin face
what puts shivers
down my spine.

I'll get the biscuits,
her voice says,
but her eyes tell me
somethin different.

Anna carries
the half-burned candle
while I balance
the silver tray
what carries the tea basket,
flowered teapot,
matchin teacup,
n two soda biscuits.

I'm careful not to bump
the large, ghosty shadows
what flicker on the wall
as we climb the stairs.

I got more thoughts
tumblin in my head'n
a mind can hold.

Anna's sweet
n fragile
as a honeycomb.

How can the Missus
be so mean?

How can anybody
be so mean?

Anna opens the Missus's door.
She uses the candle
to light two more
n nods at me to place the tray
on a small wooden table.

The Missus's bedroom
is bigger'n Mama's cabin.
Her bed's the same size
as the dinin room table,
with four carved posts
holdin up its own roof.
In all my imaginins,
I never saw a bed
with a roof
or crowded with
·so many pillows.

The Missus wears a white cap
n a wicked scowl.
How long does it take
to make a cup of tea?
Anna, bring me the chamber pot.

On the floor
beside the chamber pot
is a single rumpled blanket
what mus be
where Anna sleeps.

I turn my back
to give the Missus privacy
n pour her tea.

Brightly painted thimbles
sit in a basket
on a cushioned chair
beside the table.
I think of Mama quiltin
n mendin clothes
with pinched fingers
n swollen hands
from workin in the fields.
Would the Missus know
if I slipped a thimble
into my pocket
to give to Mama?

Grace! I'm waitin for my tea!
the Missus snarls.

I put away
my wicked thoughts.
I don't want
Mama's sweet fingers
wearin any nasty thimble
what belonged to the Missus.

A week after Jordon
runs away,
durin a breakfast
of boiled eggs n biscuits,
Master Allen announces
he'll be ridin with Moses
to place an advertisement
in the *Watchman*.
He's gettin the horses ready.

I'm sure Jordon's
out of the state by now,
the Missus says.

Master Allen looks up.
He don't say nothin
but stares at the Missus
till she turns her head.

Grace! You're slouchin,
she snaps.

I put my shoulders back,
not cause
of any promise,
but cause
I think I see
the Missus flinch,

n I know
sometimes
a mean look
stings more'n
an angry slap.

Jordon's done gone
for good,
Aunt Tempie says
later that night.
She sets down
left over crab cakes
for me, Anna,
n Uncle Moses.
No more
Master Allen's
white blindfold
for him, she says.

Uncle Moses shakes his head.
We don't know for sure, Tempie.
His ash-rimmed eyes
is sunk n sad.
Said maybe next time
he'd head for the woods.
Said he'd rather a gator
rip off his arm.
Rather the dogs
tear out his heart.
His voice is lower'n a whisper.
I heard the hounds bayin—

The woods near
the swamp? I ask,
but I might as well
be talkin to the wind.

Aunt Tempie
n Uncle Moses
pay me no mind.

Moses, no,
Aunt Tempie says.
Her voice is hushed
but firm.
*He almost made it
the last time.
He knows folks
what can help him.*
She stares at Uncle Moses
with solemn, steady eyes
what look like
they's tellin
they own story.
I feel it in my bones, Moses,
she says,
n I wonder what story
her bones know.
I wonder what story
belongs to Aunt Tempie.

Jordon's baskin in Freedom,
she says,
n I say a prayer she's right.

We eat our crab cakes
in silence,
each of us thinkin
our own thoughts
n makin our own
prayers n imaginins.

I once heared
OleGeorgeCooper
say he's seen dogs
kill a man.
Dogs'll tear your arms
right from your shoulders
n rip your nose
right from your face.
Dogs'll leave you
so broken n bloody,
you is goin to pray
the good Lord
send an angel
to shoot you.

I try to imagine
Mama's angels,
they bright,
starlight dresses
glimmerin a path
in the darkness,
they soft, silver
angel voices

whisperin messages
of hope,
they wide wings
swoopin down
n carryin Jordon
to Freedom.

But all I see
is bloodstained stars.
All I hear
is bloodthirsty howls.

Grace! Aunt Tempie snaps.
Where's your mind?
Let's clear these dishes,
n get the wood
for tomorrow's fire.

I look up.
Anna n Uncle Moses
is already gone.

Jordon's safe, Aunt Tempie
whispers, her voice kinder.
I'll wash the dishes.
You check the woodpile.

How do you know, Aunt Tempie?
How do you know Jordon's safe?
People what goes to the swamp
don't come out.
I heared OleGeorgeCooper say
if the dogs don't get em,
the gators do.

Jordon didn't go
to the swamp,
Aunt Tempie says.
He went north—
don't ask me how I know,
I jus know.

Now go outside
n check that wood.

I wonder how Aunt Tempie
knows so many things.

All I know
is she'll never tell me.

One evenin,
when Jordon's
been gone
bout two weeks,
n I'm still helpin
in the kitchen
n servin
in the dinin room,
Master Allen
tells the Missus
it's time for
a better plan.

I'm standin at the sideboard,
holdin a glass sugar bowl,
cause the Missus might need
an extra sprinkle
to sweeten her apple fritter.

Pink dots spot
the Missus's cheeks.
It was only a get-by plan.
She turns to me
with her stinkweed look
n sends me back
to the kitchen.
We obviously need someone
more experienced
and dignified,
I hear her say.

My sister and her family
will be comin
for their annual visit.
She has a big brood.

I step into the walkway,
but linger at the door,

jus listenin.

There's an auction
day after tomorrow,
Master Allen says.
I'll leave in the mornin.
When I get home
we'll send Grace
back to the kitchen.

A million yellow buttercups
burst inside me.
Wait till I tell Aunt Tempie!
Soon I'll be back in the kitchen!
Back to Saturday nights
with Mama!

And you treated him so well,
the Missus says.
I'll never understand
why he ran away.

He left me a terrible mess.
I haven't budgeted for a purchase.
I'll need to arrange a sale first.

What about that old one, Sara?
the Missus asks,
n I feel my breath get stuck
in my chest.

She's useless,
Master Allen says.
Wouldn't bring in gullyfluff.

Well then,
how about sellin Anna?
Master n the Missus
is talkin
like they's sellin
tobacco plants.

I've already told you—
Anna was a gift
from my mother.
Anna stays.

Then why not sell Grace?
A visit to the auction block
might help her learn her place.

Me? Sell me?
Feels like
a burnin fire iron
is pokin my chest,
but I stay still n listen.

Gerty, Master says,
n his voice's sharper'n
a wood splinter.
I've told you.
Grace is an investment.
Grace stays.

My breath is finally findin
its way out when
the Missus breathes
a long, lingerin sigh.

Then how about
those two little boys
who do nothin but squeal
and chase each other?

I believe they are Grace's
half brothers.

Under my feet
the floor sways,
n my head wobbles
like a spinnin top.

Toddlers—even two of em—
won't bring in enough,
I hear Master Allen say,
n I breathe deep.

The Missus's voice
rolls on
in the darkness.

Then how about sellin
their mother with them?
Bringin Grace's family
to the auction block
might finally teach Grace
who she is and
where she belongs.

Yes! Yes! Master says,
like those thoughts
is his own.
Two little ones
and their mother!
They should fetch

near enough.
We'll leave tomorrow.

The breath what's stuck
inside me
gives me a tinglin pain,
n the darkness
what's been rollin
round me
squeezes tighter
n tighter,
tighter n tighter

till I feel it
so tight
it squeezes me
inside.

I wake up
in Aunt Tempie's bed.

You done fainted,
Aunt Tempie says.
She touches my forehead.
Get some rest,
n in the mornin
you'll be fine.

I move to my pallet
n close my eyes.
In the darkness,
the chalky faces
of Master Allen
n the Missus
swirl n bulge
in a threatenin circle.

Fear sits on my bones
heavy as a barrel of lard.
Waves of sickness
roll over me.

The auction block's
a putrid place,
Uncle Jim said.
Folks is pulled n poked
like they's a prize heifer.
You hear auction,
n you run,

he said.
Auction's nothin
but weepin mamas
n whimperin children.

The auction block's no place
for my beautiful,
beautiful brothers.
The auction block's no place
for my mama what's prettiest
in the county
n what's got nothin but
the good Lord's kindness
inside her.

Aunt Tempie leaves me
to finish cleanin the kitchen
n get ready for mornin.
Master Allen's words
mix with Uncle Jim's.

They should fetch
near enough.

You hear auction,
n you run.

I'm lyin still as stone
tryin to stop the rollin
n make a plan.

They should fetch
near enough.

You hear auction,
n you run.

Round n round
I follow the words
what's runnin circles
in my achin head.

They should fetch
near enough.

You hear auction,
n you run.

Round n round
the voices go.
You hear auction,
n you run.
You run.

You run.

By the time
Aunt Tempie
returns,
my plan is set.

I pretend to be sleepin
while Aunt Tempie changes
into her nightclothes
n climbs into bed.
When her chest heaves
in a steady rhythm,
n her snore's whistlin
long n slow,
I get up.

My stomach still rolls,
but I take a breath
n keep movin
toward my plan.
I rumple my blanket
to look like I'm sleepin
n tiptoe
through the kitchen
into the dinin room.

My hands is tremblin,
but feelin my way
in the blackness,
I open the side table
n pull out
the small blue
doctorin bottle
hidden behind
Master Allen's brandy,
the blue doctorin bottle

what soothes the Missus's
delicate nerves
n helps her sleep.

I tiptoe back
into the kitchen,
ignorin the quiverin
in my bones.

I wrap left over
corn muffins
in one napkin
n dump half
the pepper jar
in another.

I push away my worries
bout Aunt Tempie
gettin blamed
for me disappearin,
or for what's missin
in the kitchen,
n quietly slip out
of the Big House
n into the night.

Forgettin the roots
n brambles what might
trip me n make me fall,
I race down the hill
n step into the moonlight
what's shelterin Mama's cabin.

Mama? I whisper.
Mama, wake up.

Grace?
Her confused n startled cry
wakes Uncle Jim,
but I hush em both
with a shake of my head
n the tap of my finger
gainst my lips.

Master Allen's plannin to sell
Thomas n Willy—
n you, I whisper.
We got to leave.

Mama blinks n rubs her eyes,
still half asleep.
Not understandin.

Master's sellin you
n Thomas n Willy!
We need to run away!
I whisper-scream.

Tonight! Now!
We need to run away!
Tomorrow first thing
he's takin you all
to the auction block!

Mama's eyes widen.

You don't jus run, Gracie,
Uncle Jim says.
It's too dangerous.
You got to have a plan.

I open the cloth napkin
n show my supplies.
We'll cover our tracks
with pepper.
We'll follow the ladle stars!

Gracie, it's not that easy!
Folks got to watch for us.

But Master's takin em
to the auction block
tomorrow!

My babies, my babies,
Mama yelps,
clutchin her chest.

Hot shame burns my face.

How can I tell her
bout all my lies n misleadins?
How I can't be trusted,
n the good Lord knows it.

How can I tell her
Master Allen is sellin her
cause the Missus
wants to teach me
my place?

How can I tell anyone
it's my fault
we need to run?

Only way to make things better
is lead em all away from here.

Mama! Please!
Tell Uncle Jim
we got to run away!
We can't let Master take you.
You said so yourself, Uncle Jim.
You hear auction,
n you run!
We need to leave—
we need to leave now!

From the corner of the cabin
comes the rustle of straw
n a soft whisper.

She's right,
Aunt Sara says.
Don't matter the reason.
We can't let Master
take any of you away.

Uncle Jim breathes deep.
He closes his eyes,
but still I see em twitchin
under his heavy lids.

If we leave now,
he finally says,
we might make it
to Cooper's swamp
before dawn.

I's stayin here,
Aunt Sara says.
I's too old.
I'll hold you back.

Uncle Jim is already up
n movin.
I'll carry you, he says.

Mama lifts Thomas
n gives him a drop
from the blue bottle.

If we go, we all go,
she says.
Nobody stays behind.

A burnin shame
shivers through me
n a dizzyin fear
swirls round my head.

What have I done?

I push through
my muzzy dark feelins—
there's no time
to think bout nothin
cept runnin away.

P A R T

T   W   O

Like hawk moths skippin
from leaf to leaf,
a wild frenzy
enters the cabin.

Rub your feet
top n bottom.

Everythin
what fits.

Not so much!

Save some to cover
our tracks.

Put this on.

Only a drop!

Pepper to throw dogs
off our scent.
Layers of clothes
to guard
gainst brambles.
Drops from the blue bottle
to keep the boys quiet.

You thought of everythin,
Aunt Sara whispers.
They can stop our voices
from speakin,
but they can't stop
our brains
from thinkin!

Shame burns a hole
in my stomach.

If the Missus
had stopped my voice
from speakin,
we wouldn't
need to run.

Uncle Jim wraps
the supplies I brought
in a rag
n ties the rag
to the walkin stick
he carved for Aunt Sara.

My heart's hammerin,
n a wamblin sickness
rolls over me,
but I keep movin.

Mama takes Willy
n I take Thomas.

Uncle Jim knots
they limp arms
round our necks
n locks they legs
round our waists.

He lifts Aunt Sara
into his arms.
Light as a goose feather,
he whispers.
Balancin the walkin stick
on his shoulder,
he looks round the cabin
n nods us outside.

Mama turns her eyes
upward.
*May the good Lord
be with us.*

Amen, we whisper
each in turn,
cept for Thomas n Willy,
already heavy with sleep.

We breathe deep
n step out of
the moon's white circle
into the shadow
of night.

Uncle Jim leads,
then comes
me n Thomas,
Mama n Willy.
We move together
in a single line,
like a lumpy caterpillar
what's lookin for a place
to lie down.

My arms already
ache with holdin,
n with every step
my braveness
drops away
like milk in
a holey bucket.

Mama's behind me,
whisperin her prayers,
n I wonder
if the good Lord n His angels
is tellin her
it's my broken promises
n haughty words
what set Master Allen
on sendin her
n my brothers
to the auction block.

You are nothin
but a slave
who needs to learn
her place,
the Missus said.

I should have listened
to Mama.
I should have kept
my eyes down
n said *Yes, ma'am,*
no, ma'am.

Aunt Sara n Uncle Jim
warned me.
Why didn't I listen?
Why didn't I listen
to Aunt Tempie
what knows her place
even if the good Lord
did make the stars
bright n beautiful
for everyone?

It don't take long
to reach the fields
n the small swamp
where I once covered
myself in mud
to make my skin
brown as Mama's.

That seems so long ago.
Long before I knew bout
blue doctorin bottles
n brandy drinks
n dishes what come
all the way from England.

Long before I knew
bout blindfolds
n ladle stars
n whippins
in the smokehouse.

Long before I understood

there's some people
what's born to rest
n some
what's born to toil.

Beyond the swamp
is the woods—
deep, dark woods
I never dared enter.

Deep, dark woods
what's filled
with wild animals
n evil spirits.

House
field
swamp.

Deep
dark
woods.

I'm steppin through
the quaggy edges
what mark my world

n wishin
I had minded
everybody's warnins.

The damp swamp air
prickles my face
n pinches neath my arms.
A branch cracks under my feet.
Somewhere bove me
an owl hoots,
n a lonesome whippoorwill
repeats his same, sad warnin.

What will Master Allen do
when he finds we's gone?

Will Aunt Tempie n Anna
be punished cause of me?

All my rightiness words
have only brought danger
to everyone I love.

My mouth's parched as dry bone.
Fear leaves a trail of tingly bumps
n a feelin like I might faint.

Mus be Mama's angels
still holdin me up,
still helpin me
carry my load.

Uncle Jim keeps movin us
deeper into darkness.
How's he knowin
which way to go?
Uncle Jim, I whisper.
*How can you see
the ladle stars?*

Uncle Jim stops in a thicket
of tall trees n low bushes.
We's not followin the stars,
he whispers.
We's findin Freedom another way.
He puts Aunt Sara down.
*Woods too deep.
Won't make it to Cooper's
before sunup.
Think I know a hidin spot—
be quicker to find
if I go alone.*

Uncle Jim tucks
us in a ditch
n covers us
with leafy branches.
Thomas whimpers
but don't wake up.

Jus hurry,
Mama whispers.

In the distance,
I hear an angry howl.
Less the Missus came lookin
for a cup of tea,
it's too soon
for dogs to be
chasin us.

Won't be gone long,
Uncle Jim says.
Gracie, you take care
of your mama.

What would Uncle Jim think
if he knew my rightiness
was the real reason
we was runnin?
Why didn't Master Allen
jus send me away?

My neck's bent into my chest
n my knees folded into my belly,
but the pain feels good
cause I deserve it.

A muddy, dull light
sifts through the branches.
Mornin birds
boss away the night
with they busy chatter.

What's takin Uncle Jim
so long?
Soon Master Allen'll
be awake.
The Missus'll be
sittin with her silver spoon
n fancy dishes what come
all the way from England.
She'll be waitin for her biscuits
while Aunt Tempie explains
Grace's still feelin a bit faint.

Or will Aunt Tempie
tell the truth?

I woke up n Grace was gone.
Haughty Grace,
what don't know her place
n won't keep her mouth shut,
has done run away!

Me n Mama
is the only ones
not sleepin.
My lies, misleadins,
n broken promises
is bumpin in my brain,
beggin me to tell Mama
the truth.

I'm so worryin bout
how to tell Mama,
I don't notice
tiny branches
cracklin
n
dry leaves
crinklin.

I don't notice
heavy
footsteps
comin
closer.

Finally from the corner
of my eye, I see
Mama's hands shake,
n my ears open
to a terrifyin scramble
of heavy, hurryin
footsteps
poundin
n scrapin
bove us.

In the distance
I hear a steady,
clatterin gallop
what makes the earth
tremble—
a heavy rhythmic
klopp, klopp
klopp, klopp
what moves closer
n closer.

Aunt Sara opens
her eyes—
Mama reaches
for my hand—
the clumpin sound's
overhead!

Klopp, klopp
klopp, klopp
SWISH!

A powerful thump
n heavy *swoosh*!
A cacklin scream
n anguished howl!

Mama squeezes
my hand.
The gallopin fades
n the earth stops
its tremblin,

but I don't.

Floatin between
the heavin crackles,

we hear
a hoarse whisper—

We need to hurry.
He's only knocked out.

My head's drownin
in panic n fear—

a wild scratchin
paws the earth—

n in one
loud,
crinkled

instant

soft copper
daylight
floods our
narrow,
dirt-packed
prison.

OleGeorgeCooper
stands bove us,
his whiskers bloomin
in the sun.
Got to hurry, he says.
Paddyroller's on our tail.
Could be a renegade,
but more'n likely he's got
a posse behind him.

Uncle Jim's already
reachin down,
helpin Mama
to her feet.

OleGeorgeCooper
lifts Aunt Sara
n places her
on a nearby log.
Stretch your bones quick,
he whispers.

Uncle Jim stoops down
n scoops up
Thomas n Willy,
still heavin in they sleep.

Squintin in the sun,
I climb myself out.

I stretch my neck
n shoulders.

I shake
the fear n tingles
from my arms n legs

n see
what I hoped
I'd never see.

Curled like a dead skunk
on the ground before me
is a scraggily,
whiskery man
wearin a hat
n fuzzy, tattered coat—
a paddyroller!

I know all bout the hate
paddyrollers carry inside,
but I never thought
I'd see one curled at my feet.
I wonder, did Master Allen
send him, or is he the kind
what goes prowlin
on his own
all hours—day n night—
jus lookin to cause trouble?

Hurry, Uncle Jim says,
handin Willy
to OleGeorgeCooper
n givin Thomas to me.
The horse got away,
but this lump'll be wakin soon.

Uncle Jim slips the rifle
from the paddyroller's arm
n gives it to Mama.

Jim, no, she says,
but he makes her
take it anyway.

Still holdin Willy,
OleGeorgeCooper unties
the rope-n-vine trap
what crossed two trees,
lifted the paddyroller
off his horse,
n thumped him
to the ground bove us.
Lucky we heard him
before he saw us, he says.
Now let's hurry!

My mouth's dry,
n fear's grindin
my bones to dust.
Is there more paddyrollers
out searchin?
Does Master Allen know?

Over n over, I hear the Missus
remindin me—
You are nothin but a slave
who needs to learn her place.
Over n over, I hear her tellin me
the folks what I love
is all in danger cause of me.

OleGeorgeCooper
leads the way,
carryin Willy in one arm
n a coil of rope-n-vine
in the other.
Mama's next,
holdin the gun
away from her body
like a dead squirrel
what's got maggots
crawlin on it.
Me n Thomas follow,
with Uncle Jim n Aunt Sara
close behind.
OleGeorgeCooper brings us
to a small stream
what rolls cool, clear water.

Drink quick, he says,
fillin his canteen.
The hidin cave's
jus beyond the marsh
n round the bend,
but we need to hurry.
Paddyroller'll be wakin soon.
Doubt he'll come lookin
without his gun,
but we don't know if he
was a loner.

Tiny fish shimmy
through the rocks
in the stream
while we quick
drink n splash our faces.

Mama cups her hands.
With eyes still closed,
the boys drink whatever water
don't leak through her fingers.

I wonder how it feels
to be a tiny fish
what flitters n darts
so free.

195

I wonder how it feels
to be the cool, clear water
what runs
without bein chased.

OleGeorgeCooper
hurries us
into the marsh.
With each step,
mud n water ooze
between my toes.

The swampy smell chokes me.
Filmy green strands of grass
cling to my legs,
n tiny insects
pinch my arms.

I keep thinkin I hear
paddyrollers
creepin behind us,
but the only sounds
is our own footfalls
n the mournful wail
of the dove.

Feels strange
to be walkin outside
in the mornin
without orders
from Aunt Tempie.

Trees hide some of the light
but still the woods
glisten
a beautiful copper yellow.

Tremblin fear
pushes us along,
till jus round the bend,
in a tangle
of maypop n nettle,
OleGeorgeCooper
turns n smiles.

See em hangin branches?
he says.
We's almost home.

Fear n guilt still grip
my bones,
but I'm breathin
the faintest scent
of Freedom,
n not all my tremblin
comes from fear.

Home is a cave
dug deep
in the canebrake,
buried neath
a bear-size tree
what's lyin on its side
n covered
in a tangle
of laurel n pine.

OleGeorgeCooper
lifts the heavy,
sweet-smellin
branches.
Welcome,
he whispers,
like he's holdin open
the door to the Big House.
Step careful.

Once we's all inside,
OleGeorgeCooper
steps in front of us
n lights a pine torch.

In all my imaginins,
I never saw a place
like this.

A few dirt steps
down from the openin's
a room almost as large
as the Missus's bedroom.

Uncle Jim don't look surprised,
but Mama squeals n starts cryin
like she did
first time I sneaked out
the Big House to see her.

Go ahead n put the boys down,
OleGeorgeCooper says,
noddin to the back corner,
where a row of pine-log beds
is lifted off the ground
n covered
with old shirts n dresses
sewed together to make a quilt.

When I put him down,
Willy opens his eyes,
but he closes em right up
when I sit beside him.

I look round.

Gainst the wall
is a tree-stump table
n four chairs

what's made of twisted
branches.
On the table is spoons
of every size
n pots n pans
with broken handles
n dented sides.

In the corner
closest to the branch-door
is another small table
what holds a crushed tinderbox
n some pieces of flint.

But most wondrous of all
is a little fireplace
made of stones n broken brick.

OleGeorgeCooper smiles.
Gets out the cold,
the wet, n the smell,
he says.

Where did all this come from?
I ask, thinkin
I could live here forever,
n wishin Anna was here too.

I got friends what help me,
OleGeorgeCooper says,

n most everyone what visits
leaves somethin behind.

Isn't we goin to stay here?
I ask.
No one will find us here.

Mama shakes her head.
This is jus a stoppin place.
We'll stay till we make a plan.

A whole pile of worms
is crawlin in my belly,
but I'd rather be here'n anywhere.

Thomas starts whinin
n wakes up Willy.
They's still too groggy
to be wild,
but anyway Aunt Sara
tries keepin em quiet
by teachin em how
to draw pictures
on the dirt floor.

OleGeorgeCooper's explainin
the hollow pipe what carries
the fireplace smoke underground
n into the swamp.
Paddyrollers always
lookin for smoke,
he says.
Can't be too careful—
though I never
had one track me here.

Finally we unwrap
our stale muffins,
sit at the table
or on the floor,
n make our own
permission to eat.

It's mornin,
but we been
walkin all night
n my body aches
to lie down.
Uncle Jim says
before anyone can rest,
we need to learn
the rules of runnin.
There's no goin out
in the daytime,
he says,
lookin at Thomas n Willy
with squinty eyes,
n no speakin
bove a whisper.

But where we goin?
What happens next? I ask.

After we get some rest,
we'll talk bout
what happens next.

Everyone settles in,
ponderin they own thoughts.
Soon, I'll have to tell Mama
bout the weevil
n Anna spillin cider
n bout what happens
in the smokehouse.

I got to tell her
the truth bout
my blackberry scratches,
n the Missus's cold fingers
what felt like fire
on my face.
I got to tell her bout
my haughty voice
what made the Missus hiss
the words still rollin
in my ears.
You are nothin but a slave
who needs to learn her place.

Not sure where my place is,
but I know it's not
the Big House.

OleGeorgeCooper
says it's still
early enough
for him to check
his traps.

What bout the paddyroller?
Mama asks.
You said yourself
he was only knocked out
n there may be others
behind him.

Not likely he'll come lookin
this far on foot,
OleGeorgeCooper says.
He's ragin,
but we got his gun.
Besides, he was a scraggily one.
Let's hope he's a loner
what's out lookin
to make trouble.

OleGeorgeCooper looks
at all of us,
but his eyes fix on Mama.
Try n get some rest,
he says kindly.
We's plenty of figurin to do
when I get back.

He nods at the far corner.
One more thing—
five long owl hoots
means danger's lurkin.
There's a narrow hollow
behind the beds.
If you hear five owl hoots,
hide till I get back,
n use em pile of rocks
gainst any
unwanted critters.

He climbs
the narrow dirt steps,
lifts the branch roof,
n slips outside.

Me n the boys
been restin all night,
Aunt Sara says
to Uncle Jim.
She pulls a string n button
from her pocket
n promises to keep
Thomas n Willy quiet.
Go on now, all of you,
get some rest.
I know what
an owl sounds like.

My body sinks
into the old-clothes quilt,
n faster'n a toad in mud,
I'm back in the forest,
followin OleGeorgeCooper.

There's a waterfall
ahead of us
gushin cold, clear water
with tiny fish
sparklin in the sun
like a rainbow.
Along the path
purple flowers twinkle.

We's almost there,
OleGeorgeCooper says,
turnin round,
n when he does,
his whiskers twitch,
n his face is whiter'n
a peeled onion.
Between two sharp
blue eyes,
a ragged scar splits open
n Master Allen's
chalky face pops out.
You left me in a terrible mess,
his angry voice hisses.
I'll find you.
I'll find you all.

I open my mouth to scream
but no words come out.
I try to run but my legs
is pinned under
a giant bear-shaped log.

I'll find you!
I'll find you!
Master's voice screams,
n when I open my eyes,
I'm tremblin
all over.

Aunt Tempie says
bad dreams
is warnins,
tellin us
what lies ahead.

Aunt Sara says
bad dreams
is nothin but
our own fears
makin faces at us
while we sleep.

I hope Aunt Sara's right.
I never want
to see Master Allen again—
not even in my dreams.

OleGeorgeCooper comes back
carryin a large, covered
wooden bowl
what smells like squirrel stew.
He smiles n shakes away
the yellow flies
what followed him inside.
Traded a new dead
for a new cooked.

Who'd you trade with?
I ask.

Uncle Jim shakes his head.
Less you know, the better,
he says, *least for now.*
He nods at Mama.
Let her rest.
Lord knows that woman's tired.
But Mama's belly wakes her,
n she opens her eyes.

OleGeorgeCooper
puts the large bowl
on the table.
There's small bowls
in that box
under the bed,
he says.

I set the table
with dented spoons
n chipped bowls
what look like they got
dropped a few times
makin they way from England.

I'm thinkin how
we brought nothin
to leave behind,
n wonderin why
the good Lord
made the world
so some folks
have pretty things
n some folks
have only things
what's used n broken.

Aunt Tempie says
you can't blame the Lord
for what people do.
Says thinkin like that
can make a mind crazy.
But I say you can't
blame a mind
for what pops into it.

We scrape the big bowl
till there's not enough
for a fly to lick,
then OleGeorgeCooper
says we got choices to make.

Go north or go deep,
he says.
He squints his gray eyes
n looks at me.
This one could pass.
Hide those curls
n she could pass.

Decision's already made,
Uncle Jim says.
We go deep.
Rather wrestle
snappers n snakes'n
keep runnin from
angry planters.

That's fine for us,
Mama says,
her voice low n serious,
but Grace here
has a chance
of escapin for real—
of livin like the good Lord

intended folks to live.
Grace has a chance
to own herself,
to learn herself letters
n how to read books,
to wear pretty dresses
n love who she wants to love
n keep what babies
is hers to keep.

Mama turns her head
n looks at me like we's
the only two people
livin.
Feels like
the rest of the world
n everyone in it
is sittin on my chest,
makin it so
I can't breathe.

I remember askin Aunt Tempie
if I could pass for white.
I was only thinkin
of buttered biscuits
n barley soup, of sweet taters
shaped like little flowers
n never worryin
bout my thoughts leakin
or bein sent to the smokehouse.
I never even had one imaginin
bout pretty dresses
or readin books n havin babies.

I sit huggin my knees.
Uncle Jim sits beside me
with Willy lyin on
his two long legs
what's stretched out
like giant logs.

Mama, Aunt Sara,
n OleGeorgeCooper
is still sittin at the table.
Already Thomas is back sleepin
in Mama's arms.

We got to give it some thought, Jim,
Mama says.
Grace has a chance for real Freedom.
We got to think bout it.

Hot prickles sting my face—
we's all sittin together
whisperin in the shadows—
with Mama wonderin
bout things
I never wondered bout.
Mama, I want to say,
don't you know
I'm the one
what brought you here?
I'm the one
what nearly sent you
to the auction block?

Don't you know?

You are nothin but a slave
who needs to learn her place,
the Missus told me.

Tell me, Mama,
do you know my place?

Feels like forever
Mama n Uncle Jim
is jus lookin at each other,
talkin with they eyes.

Could I really pass?

Aunt Tempie says
there's white folks
what is kind.

I could be kind.
I could help runaways
what need a place
to hide.
I could build
a secret room
n keep em safe
from dogs
n paddyrollers.

But what bout Mama,
Uncle Jim, n Aunt Sara?
What bout Thomas
n Willy?
Passin means crawlin
inside a lie.
Passin means makin up
a story
what won't ever be true,
n turnin all my rightiness words
to dust.

Please, Mama, I pray.
Please keep me with you.

I want my babies together,
Mama finally says.
She smiles a sad smile
what mus be happy
to keep her family
together
but sad to know
I'll never wear pretty dresses
or learn myself letters
n live the way
the good Lord
tended folks to live.

It don't matter.

I get up n hug Mama
hard as I can.

The flutterin breath
what's stuck in my chest
finally breaks free.

OleGeorgeCooper spends
the rest of the afternoon
preparin us for travel.

We'll stay close
n move only at night
when the moon is dim,
he says.
When daylight comes,
we'll rest in caves—

OleGeorgeCooper's voice
is low n rough
n puts me in mind
of tree bark what's
scratchy on the outside
but what keeps
the inside sapwood
soft n safe.

We'll cross secret trails
n hidden waterways,
followin the footpaths
of brave folks
what trudged before us.

But where we goin?
I ask,
still not understandin.

Thomas crawls into my lap
n Willy stands behind me,
playin with my hair.

Uncle Jim explains.
Beyond the canebrake
is a large lake
what's goin to take hours
to cross, he says.
On the other side of the lake
is a woods—
a big swampy woods—
what'll take days to go deep.
We'll be settlin there.

We's goin to live in the swamp?
I ask.
The Big Swamp?

Long before Thomas n Willy
was even born,
I'd heared grown-ups
spillin grave warnins
bout the Big Swamp
beyond the lake.

People what goes there
don't come out.

There's snakes n rats
n big, bitin bugs
what carry diseases
what make you die.

There's evil spirits
what suck the life
from weary travelers
n swallow the souls
of wanderin runaways.

The Big Swamp
is the devil's playground.
If he don't find you,
the paddyrollers will.

Livin in the Big Swamp
don't seem much
like Freedom.

But there's gators livin
in the swamp, I say,
coverin Thomas's ears.

I's not goin to lie,
OleGeorgeCooper says,
his voice low n serious.
There's dangers.
Bears, gators, n wildcats.
Livin in the swamp
takes courage n skill,
but if anyone's got the skill—
he looks at Uncle Jim—
he do.

Deep's the safest place
till white folks
come to they senses,
Uncle Jim says.
Lots of folks
is already livin there,
already livin in peace,
where no planter
or paddyroller
can find em.

OleGeorgeCooper nods.
Things go right,
you'll be deep
before autumn's moon.

I pull Willy round
n squeeze him
n Thomas close.

By then, Master Allen's
tobacco should be
dry n ready for bundlin.

Seems strange how little
that matters now.

It's barely been a day,
but feels like forever
since I sneaked away
from the Big House.

I wonder if the Missus
took to her bed
when she found out
I was gone.
I wonder if Anna
had to bring her
supper upstairs.
Rememberin Anna
gives me a grievin feelin,
n I ask the good Lord
to send His angels
to keep her safe.

When night falls,
Uncle Jim
n OleGeorgeCooper
leave the cave
to hunt squirrels
n forage for berries.
Thomas n Willy is asleep
on the beds,
but Mama, Aunt Sara, n me
sit at the table.

A pine-knot torch
sticks in a slit
what's carved into the table.
It casts ghosty shadows
on the cave wall.
We don't talk, but listen
for the howl of dogs
or the hoot of an owl.

Waitin n listenin
makes my heart thump
louder n heavier'n
Master Allen's
footfalls
when he's stormin.

Flickerin shadows
is makin me sleepy
when my eye
catches somethin
movin
in the darkness.

Mama, Aunt Sara!
I whisper.
Somethin long n black's
slitherin
under the beds.

Mama takes the torch
n we both tiptoe
close enough
to hear Willy's breathin
n see the dribble of sleep
what runs down his chin—
close enough
to see two cloudy-blue,
cat-shaped eyes
starin out
of a dull, dark coil.

A snake!

The blackest, fattest,
meanest-lookin snake
I ever seen!

He raises his head
n opens his mouth.
Two long fangs
hang in a cave
of white cotton.
A low crinklin sound
like footsteps on
dry leaves
scratches the dark,
n a musty scent
like spoiled fruit
chokes me.

Willy sits up
n rubs his eyes.
What's that smell?

Go back to sleep, Willy,
I whisper,
you is jus dreamin.

I feel Aunt Sara's
hand on my shoulder.
Step back, Grace.
Slow as you can,
step back.

My legs is weaker'n
swamp grass,
but I step back.

So does Mama.
The snake closes
his mouth
n lowers his head.

My whole self's
tremblin—
inside n out.

That snake's holdin a poison
what could kill us,
Aunt Sara says.
But he'll stay put
if we leave him be.

Willy's already back to sleep,
but Mama's eyes
is wide as hickory nuts.
What bout my boys?

Every creature's got a voice,
Aunt Sara says,
n this snake's already told us
he's ready to fight.
The boys'll be fine
long as they stay sleepin.

Did you see his blue eyes?
Mama asks.

Did you ever see a snake
with blue eyes?

Aunt Sara guides Mama
to her chair
n puts the pine-knot torch
back in the slit.

Mus be gettin ready
to shed his skin,
she says.
We'll keep watch.
Sometimes bein brave
is jus knowin
when to step back
n wait.

228

Willy wakes up again.
Mama, he calls.
Mama, I smell somethin.
He sits up n
scrunches his nose.

It's nothin, baby,
go back to sleep.
Mama tries
to keep her voice happy,
but I can hear
the shake in it.

Willy dangles his foot
over the side of the bed.

Stay on the bed!
Mama screams,
n Willy starts to cry.

Mama takes the torch
n walks toward him real slow.
Shhh, don't cry,
stay in bed!
Mama's comin!

In the dim light
of the pine torch,
we see the snake
uncoil.

He points his
arrow-shaped head
toward Mama.
He opens
his cotton mouth.

He slithers
toward her.

Mama, Mama!
Willy calls,
wakin up Thomas.

Mama! Mama!
they both call.

Shhh . . .

Mama walks
toward the bed.
The snake slithers
toward Mama.

I's here!
Mama tells
the boys,
fear swallowin
her words.

The snake
holds his
angry head
high,
n I see
the Missus
standin over me—
I feel her
cold hands—
n smell her

snarlin
oyster breath.

In the white
hollow
of the snake's
stretched
mouth,
his sharp fangs
flash.

Aunt Sara pops up
n taps her cane.

The snake turns
n before
my thoughts
shape into sense,
I grab a rock,
move past Mama,
n drop it
on the snake's
gapin head.

Keep your mouth closed!
I scream,
much louder'n I should.

Keep your mouth closed!

Blood squirts
from the snake's
crushed skull,
but he still squirms.

Mama rushes
to the bed
n takes Willy
into her arms.
Thomas wriggles
beside her,
n her arms open
to hold him too.

Hush, little babies,
Mama sings,
but her voice
withers into rasps.

At my feet,
the snake
twitches n turns—

Leave it be,
Aunt Sara says.
Those white fangs
still got poison in em.
Even dead, a snake
what's got venom
can kill.

The coiled snake
puts me in mind
of the paddyroller
we left
layin
in the woods.

Even knocked out,
them what's got venom
can kill.

Finally Uncle Jim
comes in carryin
a bundle of berries
n a basket what smells
like heaven.
What have we here?
he asks.

Aunt Sara tells him
how I dropped the rock
n killed the snake,
how I saved Mama
n maybe Willy.

OleGeorgeCooper takes
another rock
n severs the snake's head
completely.
Usin the tip of Aunt Sara's
walkin stick,
he pushes the snake head
into a wooden bucket
n brings it outside to bury.
The rest of the snake
still wriggles n squirms.

Uncle Jim lifts the snake
by its tail
n drapes it cross
the hearth.

Aunt Sara shakes her head.
No brains but still strikin out.

Master Allen thinks
Aunt Sara's useless,
but she's not.
Aunt Sara's too weak
to walk far
n too tired
to give the boys
a breeze when it's hot,
but she's not useless.
Aunt Sara knows stuff.
Sometimes knowin stuff's
as important as doin stuff.

Everybody's got a worth.

Late that night,
when the snake finally
stops twitchin,
OleGeorgeCooper
skins it n drops
a rope of flesh
into a pot of boilin water.
Not as good as
pork biscuits,
but an empty belly
don't care.

I'm glad my belly's full
of biscuits n berries
stead of a poison snake
what puts me in mind
of the Missus
n the paddyroller.

Tempie left the basket
at the edge
of the woods,
OleGeorgeCooper says.
Good I got friends
what take care of me
n my travelers.

Tempie? My Aunt Tempie?
Aunt Tempie's been helpin
OleGeorgeCooper care
for runaways?
Aunt Tempie what works
in Master Allen's Big House?

OleGeorgeCooper nods.
Tempie's been helpin me
a long time, he says.

My Aunt Tempie
what tells me
to mind my own business
n not talk back—
what gets up in the dark
n goes to bed when it's darker—
my Aunt Tempie what makes
fancy tater flowers
for the Missus
n blackberry syrup
for Master's brother?

My Aunt Tempie's been
helpin runaways?

OleGeorgeCooper nods
n smiles.
The very same.

How could that be?
I thought Aunt Tempie
didn't care
bout nothin cept
makin Master Allen
n the Missus happy.
How could I be so wrong?

My face burns
in wonder n shame.
I judged Aunt Tempie
same as the Missus
judged me.

When the boys is asleep,
OleGeorgeCooper tells us
bout the secrets tucked
inside Aunt Tempie's basket.

*I didn't know
bout Aunt Tempie,* I say.

*Less the children know,
the better,* Uncle Jim says.
But now it's time to grow up.

I watch Thomas n Willy
curled together on the bed
like baby kittens.
Seems they's too young
to grow up.

Age don't make you old,
Aunt Sara says, *worries do.*

I take a deep breath.
I got more worries'n
a swamp's got flies.

Nobody knows
it's my broken promises
n sassy words
what got the Missus
set on sendin Mama

n the boys away.
Nobody knows
how I judged Aunt Tempie
n never thanked her
for all the good things
she done.

If worries make you old,
I mus be older'n Aunt Sara.

OleGeorgeCooper
takes out a small flat rock
what's buried
in the bottom
of the basket.

Mean anythin?
he asks me.

I shake my head.

Look careful, he says,
n tell me what you see.

I hold the rock
up to the torch
n look close.

Scratched into
the smooth stone
is an egg-shaped circle
with another circle inside.
A curved line
what looks like the moon
is scratched into
the top corner.

That looks like the moon,
I say,
n that looks like a fish.

OleGeorgeCooper nods.
That is the moon.
But that's not a fish.
That's an eye.
Aunt Tempie's warnin us
to stay put.

He looks at Uncle Jim.
Guess the paddyrollers
is back huntin tonight.

The worms what's been
crawlin in my belly
feel like they's
eatin my bones.
Everyone's in danger
cause of me.

Not sure what this is,
OleGeorgeCooper says
n he pulls out
a worn
strip of cloth
what I recognize
right away.

That's mine! I say,
n a sorrowin shame
sinks inside me.

Mama ties the ribbon
round my wrist.
Seems Aunt Tempie
is sendin you a message,
she says.

I remember Aunt Tempie
liftin my chin n tellin me
the good Lord didn't need
a ribbon to hear our prayers.
I remember her pullin

the pallet from under her bed
n tuckin Mama's ribbon
into the hem of my blanket.

What we love
is tied to us forever,
I say, n add
a silent prayer
to the good Lord
n His angels.
Please keep watch over
my Aunt Tempie
n forgive me
for misjudgin her.

For the next few nights,
OleGeorgeCooper's
the only one
what goes outside.

The crickets n frogs
never stop chirpin,
n it seems like
it's always night.
Seems like
we'll be hidin
forever.

Only OleGeorgeCooper
knows for sure
when the sun's gone
n the moon's out,
n when OleGeorgeCooper
thinks it's safe enough,
he disappears
like a turtle
slippin into
murky water.

Each time he leaves,
he brings back
somethin to eat.
It's too dangerous
for Aunt Tempie
to leave stale muffins

or scratched rocks,
but even in the dark,
OleGeorgeCooper knows
where to find
the pine nuts
n the pawpaw trees.

Hardest part
of the wait
is keepin
Thomas n Willy
from laughin too loud.
There's not much room
to run round,
but silliness squeezes
in the smallest space.
Mama tries makin a game
of keepin quiet,
but the hush
don't last long.

Let's draw, I say,
n in the flickerin
pine light,
me n the boys
make pictures
on the dirt floor.

Thomas's jus scratchin,
but Willy starts makin
circles n squiggily lines
what look like people—
Uncle Jim, tallest of all,
wearin somethin on his head
what mus be the hat
he wears in the field,
n next to him

Mama n Aunt Sara,
both jus skinny lines
with circles on top,
cept Aunt Sara's
got three legs
what mus be her cane.
Even OleGeorgeCooper's there,
standin next to Aunt Sara,
his circle face marked
with sharp lines n scratches.

In a small space
bove Uncle Jim's hat,
I add three circles
n some short lines—
That's us, I say,
n Willy laughs.

Aunt Sara rests
an angry look on us,
but Willy
don't notice
n starts
crossin his eyes,
n twistin his tongue
so Thomas
spits out all
the tied-up giggles
he's been holdin in.

uple of days n nights
n nothin to eat but berries
als the loudness
om Thomas n Willy
better'n all of Uncle Jim's
sharp shushes
n Aunt Sara's squinty frowns.

Last time OleGeorgeCooper
was out,
so were the dogs,
so even he's been stayin put.
Our pawpaw n berry basket's
jus bout empty.

We is starvin to death,
n it's my fault.
If it weren't for me
n my rightiness,
Uncle Jim would be singin
in our moonlight garden,
n Mama n the boys
would be eatin left over muffins
n johnnycakes,
stead of starvin in a cave
what's got poison snakes
hidin in every corner.

Got to risk a run, Uncle Jim says.
Boys got to eat. Grace too.

Be quiet!
Uncle Jim hisses
from the corner
where's he's
skinnin a squirrel.

Little ones is supposed to
laugh n have fun,
Mama snaps,
but she shushes
us anyway.
Tears well in her eyes.
Not natural keepin
little ones so quiet,
she says to me.

Worryin n waitin
wraps round
our bones
like swamp fog.

Everybody's got to eat, I say.

OleGeorgeCooper
shakes his head.
Still too dangerous.

But we been inside for days,
I say.
Maybe the dogs moved on.
Maybe Aunt Tempie left
another basket.
How will we even know?

Seems guilt n hunger's
liftin the fog
from my brain,
n thoughts what's been lyin
faint for so long
tumble n spill.
We got to do somethin!
We can't jus wait
for paddyrollers or dogs
to find us!
We can't jus starve to death!
We got to take a chance!

Grace! Mama says,
movin from the table
to the bed where I'm sittin.
Her eyes look like they's

sinkin into her skull.
Grace, you got to trust
the good Lord, she says.
We need to be patient
awhile longer.

Lookin into those hungry eyes
what's still floatin so much love
makes somethin inside me crumble.

But, Mama, I cry,
it's my fault we had to run.
I didn't keep my promises.
I didn't keep my eyes down.
I didn't keep my mouth shut.
I made the Missus mad
n she would've sent me
to the smokehouse
but Miss Charlotte was there
so she sent me
to the blackberry patch
n Jordon helped me
but made me get scratches
anyway
cause the Missus
would be lookin for em
n he was right.

My thoughts leak
faster'n spilled cider.

She wanted Master Allen
to bring me
to the auction block,
but Master Allen said no
cause I was a vestment.
That's when the Missus
told Master Allen
to sell Thomas n Willy.
Only toddlers don't
fetch enough money
so the Missus told him
to sell you too.
Said he'd get more money
if you was sold with em
n sellin you would learn me
who I am n where I belong
cause I'm haughty, Mama,
n don't know my place.
If I kept my mouth shut
n my eyes down,
Uncle Jim would be tendin
our moonlight garden,
n we'd all be eatin
food what's left over
from the Big House.
I broke my promise.
The good Lord knows
I can't be trusted,
n now He don't care.
Now we is all starvin

n maybe goin to get caught—
or even die—

Mama draws me close.
Her gown smells damp
n swampy, but still
she smells like Mama,
n I stop talkin
to catch my breath
n breathe in
Mama's kindness.
My sweet, sweet Grace,
she says.
Some folks don't need
a reason to hate.

But—

Shhh, Mama says.
Hatin's a choice
what's got nothin
to do with you.

But if I kept my promises—
if I didn't talk back—
if I kept my eyes down—

I was wrong to keep you
from lookin at the stars,
Mama says,
kissin my hair

n restin her head on mine.
That's where the good Lord
n His angels live.
That's where hope
shines her beautiful face.

Uncle Jim sits on
the other side of me.
Gracie, he says, *I'd rather*
be eatin worms I dug myself 'n
scraps from Allen's table.
He looks at OleGeorgeCooper.
Maybe Grace is right.
Maybe we need to take a chance.

I'll go, OleGeorgeCooper says.
I won't go far, but I'll go.

The good Lord's
love n forgiveness
wrap round me,
n some of my
shameful feelins
start meltin away—
but my family's still
in danger
cause of me,
n guilty, ghosty
worries
linger.

Uncle Jim's still searchin
the cave for critters
when OleGeorgeCooper
comes back carryin
Aunt Tempie's basket.
Our bellies been fillin
with nuts n berries so long
the smell of Big House food
makes my stomach jump.

Still warm n no maggots,
OleGeorgeCooper says.
Tempie mus've jus left it.

Before we finish devourin
our ham n johnnycakes,
he pulls out a flat gray rock
what's got scratches in it—
two wavy lines like
the ruffle on Anna's collar.
That's water, he explains.
*Tempie's tellin us
it's safe to leave.*

He looks at me.
Good we took the chance.

Uncle Jim pushes
our food away.
Tonight's the night.

He n Mama jump up
n bundle the boys
in they extra shirts.
Aunt Sara gives em
they spoonful of quiet.
I rewrap our dinner.

Now there's no room
in our bellies for food.

Now we is all of us
stuffed with fear.

OleGeorgeCooper reviews
the rules he's been spoutin
every night.

No matter what you see
slitherin beside you,
no matter what you feel
creepin up your leg
or crawlin long your neck,
no matter what you hear
buzzin in your ears,
keep quiet, keep movin!
I'll be leadin,
so follow close—
I see any snakes
or gators,
I'll give em a wide berth—
you do the same.
They won't bother you
if you give em space.

OleGeorgeCooper talks
slow n low n serious.

You is goin to gag
on the stink,
n feel like faintin
from fear,
but you got to
keep quiet
n keep movin.

Them what makes it
to Freedom is braver'n
snakes, gators, or bitin flies.

He nods real solemn.

There's nothin in the swamp
what's worse'n
the stink
of bein a slave.

OleGeorgeCooper lifts
little Willy into his arms
n Uncle Jim reaches
for Aunt Sara.

You take Thomas,
Aunt Sara says.
I's stayin here.
She looks at OleGeorgeCooper.
That's if you'll let me stay.
Aunt Sara's shoulders is
narrow n bent,
but she sets her back
strong as Uncle Jim's.
I don't eat much,
n I can keep out the snakes
n other critters what comes in
while you is out.
I can protect runaways what
stop n hide here too.
They'll be lonesome n afraid.
I can give em a kind word
n the courage to keep goin.

OleGeorgeCooper nods.
Be pleased to have the help.
Besides, the road ahead's
difficult n dangerous—
you is safer here.

Everyone agrees
Aunt Sara should stay.
Even Mama.
It's your choice, Aunt Sara,
she says, her voice steady n soft.
It's your choice.

Mama! I thought you said
we stay together?
I turn to Aunt Sara.
Don't you want to stay with us?
Don't you want to keep
goin on to Freedom?

Aunt Sara brushes my face
with her twisted, bony hand.
My sweet child, she says,
I done found my Freedom.
Don't you hear
your mama talkin?
It's my choice.
She looks at Mama,
then again at me.
In all my years,
I never had
my own choice.

Aunt Sara n Mama
hold each other
a long time.

There's no words,
Mama finally whispers.

Aunt Sara touches
Mama's face with her
knotty hands.
May the good Lord keep you,
she says.

Uncle Jim nods at Aunt Sara,
his solemn eyes tellin her good-bye,
n promisin her
he'll take good care of us.
He tugs Mama's shoulders.
Come on, Catherine,
he whispers, *we need to go.*

It's my turn to say good-bye
n I wrap my arms tight
round Aunt Sara's waist
to keep my sorrow
from spillin out.

Aunt Sara reaches
into her pocket n pulls out
a tiny porcelain button.
She presses it into my hand.
Remember me, Grace—
fight gainst em
what thinks they own you.

Any way you can,
fight gainst em.

I won't ever forget you,
I whisper.
I put the button
into my torn pocket,
n tie Mama's ribbon
round Aunt Sara's narrow wrist.

Aunt Sara smiles,
tears softenin the crust
what's always stuck
in the corner of her eyes.

Let's go, OleGeorgeCooper says.
He nods at the gun
standin in the corner.
Only if you have to, Sara.

Uncle Jim lifts Thomas
into his arms.
Silent, we file past Aunt Sara.
Blessins, she whispers,
kissin her hand n touchin
each of us as we pass.

Grief quivers inside me
like a butterfly
what's dyin in the grass.

Outside, a silver,
shadowy moon
flickers
behind the clouds.
A heavy mist
wraps its dark arms
round us.

The air smells like
pine n wet bark.
OleGeorgeCooper leads us,
carryin Willy like a tobacco sack
wrapped round his neck.
Uncle Jim's next with Thomas.
Then there's me,
holdin whatever wrapped-up
supplies is left—
a handful of berries,
a slice of ham,
some johnnycake crumbs,
n an almost-dry bottle
of blue sleep.
Behind me,
I hear Mama
whisperin,
askin the good Lord
to help carry
her heavy heart.

I pray too.
I beg the good Lord
to keep away the dogs,
paddyrollers,
n snakes.
I beg Him
to watch over
Aunt Sara
n guide us
on our way
to Freedom.

Seems Mama's prayers
is soft silver threads
leadin straight to the stars,
leadin right to the place
where the good Lord
n His angels
listen n keep watch.

My prayers
is like Aunt Sara's button—
too small n cracked
to hold anythin together
but a broken heart.

The good Lord don't care
bout fancy words,
Mama said
when she taught me
to pray.
You jus give Him
your thoughts
any which way you can.
He'll listen n
hold em safe.

Tiny glimmers
of moonlight
shimmer on the path
like angel wings,
n I know

the good Lord's tryin
to send me slivers
of hope.

But my family's
still in danger.

Much as I try
to leave it
behind,
a quiverin
shadow
of sorrow
n shame
follows me.

We move so quiet
seems we is like all
the other creatures
livin in the woods.
Seems we is part
of the woods,
part of the darkness
what covers us,
part of a pure,
unspoiled world—
a different world'n
the one Master Allen
n the Missus live in.
Not a world
of shiny silver
or fancy dishes
what come
all the way
from England,
not a world
of whips, lashes,
n angry words—

but a different world.

Even in the darkness,
with creaky
night sounds
what frighten me,
n a tremblin fear

of snakes
what might be hidin
in the grass,
even with
broken buttons,
n sad good-byes,
even with my
quiverin shame,

I feel part
of another world,
a beautiful world,
a world
what whispers
Freedom.

We walk a long time.

The only sounds
is soft n ghosty—

tiny crackles
neath our feet,
Mama's silvery
whispers,

the flap of wings
in dark branches,
n the tiny hoots
n chitters
of unseen creatures.

I feel em
all round me
like the good Lord's angels,
watchin over us,
n coverin our tracks.

Under my feet,
the earth begins
to soften.

Cane's thick here,
OleGeorgeCooper explains.
Goin to have to crouch or crawl.
You'll be fine
if you keep movin.
We all need
to keep quiet
n keep movin.

I feel the earth tuggin
at my feet,
the giant stalks reachin
to grab hold of me,
n wonder if evil spirits
is already makin ready
to swallow my soul.

Keep movin,
Mama whispers.

Keep movin,
I repeat.

Finally we stand
at the edge
of a large pond
of stinkin water
what mus be full
of snakes, flies,
snappin turtles,
n fearsome gators.

Got to keep movin,
OleGeorgeCooper says.
Daylight's comin fast.
He heads into water
what reaches jus below
Willy's saggin body.

I hold my breath
n step into
the warm, buggy,
foul-smellin pond.

Beside me,
my gown billows
like dirty clouds.
Everywhere,
mosquitoes buzz
n bite.

Under the water,
somethin
soft n slimy
wraps round
my bare legs.

I hold my breath
n keep movin.

We wade along, slow
n even-stepped,
till without warnin,
OleGeorgeCooper
changes direction.
It feels like we's
circlin backward
n fear takes hold
of me.

Uncle Jim steps aside
n nods for me
to fill the watery gap.
I turn round jus enough
to see him
slip behind Mama.

Don't be afraid,
I hear him whisper.
It's eyein somethin else.
It won't bother us
if we don't bother it.

Bother who?
The only sound's
the soft plop
n splash of water,
the snap
n flick of bugs
nippin at the darkness.

There's nothin round me
but my own fears
growin like mushrooms
after a storm,

n then,
I see what looks like
a large log
glidin next to us.

Plonk! the log turns—

n starin straight at me
is a large snubby snout
what's got two orange eyes
shinin like circles of fire,
n a row of pointy teeth
what's waitin
to devour us all.

OleGeorgeCooper
keeps movin wide,
payin the gator no mind,
but I'm feelin faint,
ready to slide
underwater
n disappear.

Keep movin,
Mama whispers
in an angel voice.
Don't look.

But I do look

n I do see.

Hangin from
the gator's mouth

is a bushy ringed tail
n two danglin paws.

Keep quiet n keep movin.

I'm only talkin to myself,
but it feels
like I'm prayin
n the good Lord's answerin.

By the time we step
out of the pond,
daylight streams
through the treetops.

My dress sticks
to my skin.
My arms ache n itch.

Clusters of welts,
as wide as walnuts
n red as cherries,
form a wobbly
ladder on my leg.

OleGeorgeCooper
leads us to a small cave
covered with branches, sticks,
n a sheet of moss
thick as the rug
in the Missus's bedroom.

Thomas n Willy is still
too drowsy to eat,
but Mama forces em
to nibble the last
of the berries,
n we lie down
in straw what mus be
crawlin with chiggers.

Before I know it,
OleGeorgeCooper
is standin over me,
tellin me it's nighttime.

Time to wake up.
Time to move on.

The blue bottle's
almost empty,
but Mama mixes
whatever's left
with drops of water
from the canteen
OleGeorgeCooper
keeps strapped to his belt.

Don't need much, he says.
We's not far from the lake.
Dogs'll lose the scent,
n paddyrollers won't cross
less they's already been trackin.

Mama hurries me along,
but it feels like
iron chains is
bindin my legs.

We slog for hours
till finally the path
begins to widen
n we walk side by side.

Moonlight glistens
on a dark lake
what's set before us
like a shimmerin
piece of fallen sky.

OleGeorgeCooper
flips over a log
lyin at the water's edge.

Hidin in plain sight,
he whispers.

He smiles n nods,
helpin each of us
step careful
into a carved-out
bark canoe.

With a soft *plink*
n quiet ripple,
OleGeorgeCooper slips
the canoe
into the water
n climbs inside.
He sits at one end
n Uncle Jim
sits at the other.
Mama n me
sit in the middle,
holdin Thomas
n Willy.

Mama puts her hand
on my shoulder.
Be brave, Grace,
she whispers,
but ghosty words
n warnins
seem to rise
from the dark water—

People what goes
to the Big Swamp
don't come out.

There's snakes n rats
n big, bitin bugs.

There's evil spirits
what swallow the souls
of wanderin runaways—

Fear chokes me
like the devil himself
is catchin hold
of my throat.

Silent as moonlight
we glide
into the forever water.

OleGeorgeCooper
guides the canoe
round a narrow bend,
windin us
farther away
from the riverbank,
farther away
from Mama's cabin
n the Big House,
from Master Allen
n the Missus,
farther away
from Aunt Sara
n Aunt Tempie,
from Anna
n Uncle Moses,
farther away
from everythin
I ever knew.

Farther n farther
into darkness
we drift,
till before long,
we disappear too.

Far off,
a solitary cypress
keeps watch,
its ghosty silhouette
risin from
the dark water.

The only sounds
is the distant,
lonesome squawks
of the night heron,
the tiny swash n ripple
of our canoe,
n the soft,
silver prayers
Mama's sendin
to heaven.

Bove me,
the stars sparkle
low n bright.
I reach in my pocket
n squeeze Aunt Sara's small,
broken button.

I listen to the quiet
n wonder
what new world
is waitin.

PART

T H R E E

When we reach the other side
of the lake, an old man
in a coonskin cap—
what looks like a runaway—
points a shotgun at us.
Who goes there? he says.

Feels like my blood's
rushin out of me—
have we really come so far
jus to be killed?

The passengers you been
waitin for,
OleGeorgeCooper says.
Five of em.

The old man puts down
his shotgun,
n my breath,
weak as a feather,
flutters out.
Settlement's a few days' trek from here.
There's folks been waitin for you.

I wonder if folks know bout us
the same way Aunt Tempie
knew bout Jordon bein safe.
I feel it in my bones, she said,
n I imagine

Freedom's twistin trail
scattered
with ribbons,
bones,
n ladle stars
what's gathered
by the good Lord's angels
n given back
to fearless runaways.

Uncle Jim shifts Thomas
in his arms
n turns to OleGeorgeCooper.
My family, he starts to say,
but his voice has a quiver in it
what I never heared before,
n a small whistlin sob
scrapes out of his throat.

We's all one family, Jim,
OleGeorgeCooper says.
He squeezes Uncle Jim's shoulder.
You's a good man, I wish you well.

Thank you for everythin,
Uncle Jim whispers.

*May the good Lord
protect you always,*
Mama says,

tears shimmerin her words too.
Tell Sara she's in our hearts.

OleGeorgeCooper gives Willy
to Mama.
Soon you's goin to run free,
little man,
he says,
his hands on Willy's head.

It's my turn to say
good-bye,
but the words
what's always runnin
circles in my head
tiptoe away.

You is a brave little lady,
OleGeorgeCooper says.
Keep your head n your heart
on what's right n good,
n be proud of who you is.

I look into his scarred face
what used to scare me,
n it seems to me
the good Lord's
already makin it beautiful.
Thank you, I whisper,
huggin him tight.

Tell Aunt Sara we is safe.
Tell her I won't ever forget her.

OleGeorgeCooper pulls away,
nods at each of us,
n turns to go.

Ask Aunt Tempie to tell
Anna n Uncle Moses
we made it cross the lake,
I whisper-call.

OleGeorgeCooper turns again
n smiles.
They'll be pleased to hear it.
He gives us one last nod.
Stay alert—be strong—
you'll find your way.

Then he climbs
back in the canoe,
n we watch him
drift away.

Seems to me
the road to Freedom
is marked
with too many
sad good-byes.

The old man
in the coonskin hat
pulls us from our
sad partin thoughts
with a loud cough.

We best get movin,
he says.
He shows us
what markins
to follow,
what crossed branches
lead to trails,
what piles of brush
conceal hidin spots.

He stays with us
till first light.
You'll be safe
long as you stay
the course,
he says.
The path will lead
to a swell in the ground.
You'll see a circle
of mud-n-log huts
surroundin a pile
of stacked brush.
That's the settlement.

Anybody ask,
say Rainbow Joe sent you.

Rainbow Joe nods
n disappears into the forest.
I wonder where he goes
n where he's been.
I wonder how many secrets
this old swamp holds.

When a bright mornin sunlight
quivers through the trees,
we slip into a hollow space
inside a ring
of ancient cypresses.

Jus as I'm bout to fall asleep,
I hear Mama
whisper somethin
bout angels
what's wearin
coonskin caps.

After three days
restin in the sun
n three nights
travelin neath the stars,
the earth grows drier,
n the smell of
smoked meat
floats amid
the musty scent
of dried leaves n bark.

Safe enough to keep walkin
in daylight,
Uncle Jim says
in a voice
softer'n moonlight.
Mama gives him
a weak smile.

We been eatin
nothin but roots
n berries for days.
The boys is
light as gullyfluff
n jus as quiet.
We's all jus too tired.
Seems even my lingerin
guilt n shame is
nothin more'n weary shadows.

Been so long
since we walked
in daylight,
the mornin sun
feels strange,
n my eyes pinch
n struggle
to see clear.

*Think this path leads
to the settlement,*
Uncle Jim says, givin
Thomas to Mama.

The worries n fears
what's been too worn out
to trouble me
wake up.
I shift Willy
to my other arm
n send the good Lord
a quick prayer.
Keep us safe, I whisper.
Please.

We follow a trail upward
to a circle of huts—
some of em small n round,
n some of em
what look like our cabin,
cept they's sittin on stilts.

The camp is empty
but for a boy
what looks a few years
older'n me
n a man wearin
ragged pants n a feather vest—
both of em standin guard
by a pile of brush.
The man approaches
n asks our business.

Rainbow Joe sent us,
Uncle Jim says,
stretchin out his hand.

Welcome, the man says.
Name's Samuel.
Spected you days ago—
was gettin worried.
He nods at the boy
standin beside him.
This here is Brooklyn.

Brooklyn's skin is dark
as a crow's wing,
n a scar
curved like the moon
slashes cross
his right eye.
He nods
n shakes Uncle Jim's hand.

I never heared
a name like Brooklyn,
but in all my wonderins,
I never imagined
a place like this either.

I never imagined
this small
circle of cabins
surrounded by tall trees
n tangled branches.

Most of the cabins
have gardens
with neat rows
n mounds
of green plants
growin behind
twisted vine fences.

Some of em
have racks
with clothes
n furs
dryin in the sun.

A simple wagon
made of logs
n braided vines
sits in front of
the smallest cabin,
n a cloth cradle
hangs between
two shelterin trees.

300

This looks like a place
where folks come to live—
not like a place
where folks come to hide.

For the first time
in a long time,
the worms
what's been
rollin n twistin
in my belly
make room
for a scantlin
of hope.

Uncle Jim tells Samuel
bout the paddyroller
what kept us hidin
n slowin our pace.
Then he introduces us.
This here's our Grace—
wasn't for her,
we'd be bundlin tobacco.

Uncle Jim's voice
sounds proud,
n I feel lifted up
like Thomas n Willy
mus feel when Uncle Jim
lifts em to the moon.

A woman in a tattered dress
patched with fur
comes outside.
Samuel, she scolds, *these folks*
mus be tired n hungry!
You can talk inside.

Maddie's right, Samuel says.
He nods at Brooklyn.
You stay n keep lookout.

We follow Samuel n Maddie
into a small, clean cabin
what's got fur rugs on the floor

n a table, bench, n bed
made from logs.

Maddie brings each of us a bowl
of muskrat stew
n a carved wood spoon.

I'm still holdin Willy,
but he finally lets go,
dips his spoon
into the stew, n starts slurpin.
Mama closes her eyes
n reaches out to squeeze
my hand.
I know she's thankin
the good Lord for bringin us here.
I close my eyes n thank Him too.

*Paddyrollers don't usually
come this far,* Samuel says,
but if they do, we'll be ready.
He nods to a stack of bows,
arrows, rocks, n guns.

Maddie shakes her head.
*Been livin here more'n two years.
Never seen a paddyroller
what's brave enough to come this far.*

But you best beware, Samuel says,
when the wildcats is hungry—
they come close—
n we jus lost a good man
to a bear protectin her cub.

We won't let our guard down,
Uncle Jim says,
n a cold fear grips me again.
Will livin with wildcats n bears
really will be better'n livin
in the Big House?

You'll make it, Samuel says.
There's natives been livin
in these woods for years.

I clutch the broken button
in my pocket
n think of Aunt Sara.

Livin in a cave
or deep in the wild
don't seem much
like Freedom,

but neither is livin in fear
of fiery words n whippins.

Maddie offers Mama,
me, n the boys
a place to lie down
while Samuel
shows Uncle Jim
the surroundin woods.
After three nights
of little sleep,
Mama's grateful,
but my mind's
swarmin with thoughts
what need ponderin.

*I'll sit outside
with the boys,* I say.
Mama's scared
to let us go,
but Maddie promises
it's safe.

*We'll be jus outside
the cabin, Mama.*

Willy takes my hand,
but Thomas clings to Mama.
Neither boy makes a sound,
n I wonder if I'll ever hear em
talk or laugh again.

I sit on the ground
outside Maddie's cabin,

n Willy starts drawin
a picture in the dirt—
same picture he always draws—
circles n lines
what look like people—
Uncle Jim, tallest of all,
n next to him,
Mama n Aunt Sara
n OleGeorgeCooper,
with his scratchy face,
n me n Thomas n Willy
with our big circle heads
n short-line legs.

Daylight n sleep
is pinchin my eyes,
but I try sortin my thoughts.
Have we really
escaped Master Allen?
Is OleGeorgeCooper
back with Aunt Sara?
Is he already helpin
other runaways?

Am I really outside
ponderin
in the light of day?

Is this Freedom?

I watch Brooklyn
watchin the woods
n camp.
He catches my eye
n walks over.
Willy crawls into my lap.

I'm glad you arrived safely,
Brooklyn says.

I'm glad too, I say.

Brooklyn smiles
n his scar crinkles
into his eyes,
givin me
a kindliness feelin
what makes me want
to be his friend.

I never heared
a name like Brooklyn,
I say,
hopin he'll linger awhile.

Brooklyn puffs out
his chest.
I named myself
when I got here,
he says.

Brooklyn's a place up north.
My mama told us
there's a place in Brooklyn
where folks like us
go to their own school
and church.
They even buy land
and vote.
His shoulders droop.
My daddy set out to find it
but never came back.
Twice I tried
to get there myself,
and twice I got caught.

I'm sorry, I say.
I think of Jordon
n hope he really did
make it north,
maybe even to Brooklyn.
How did you end up here?

My third try, Master
set the hounds after me,
Brooklyn says.
He forgot I was the one
who cared for them.
I knew them all by name,
and they heeded me
same as they heeded him.

The dogs let me
escape into the woods.
I was hiding there
when a man named Cooper
found me. He took me
across the lake with Samuel.

Brooklyn stops talkin
n smiles.
Mighty glad
you made it here safe,
he says again.
He pats Willy's head.
And you too, Willy.

308

Brooklyn looks at me,
One day, you can tell me
your story.

Brooklyn limps back
to his spot
by the pile of brush,
leavin me to ponder
my own story.

When Uncle Jim
comes back,
him n Samuel
start talkin to Brooklyn.
I watch em nod n point
to the woods
n wonder
what they's sayin.

Papa, Willy whispers,
squirmin out of my lap
n runnin to Uncle Jim.

I follow close behind.
I'm going to help
your papa
build your cabin,
Brooklyn says.

He's not—
I start to say,
but stop myself.

Uncle Jim smiles.
There's already six families
livin here, he says.
Best to spread out.
There's a small clearin
cross the stream.
Samuel says

Brooklyn's got skills
what will help us build.

Fragile as a turnip sprout,
my scantlin of hope
stretches to the sun.

*Think I'll take you up
on that rest,*
Uncle Jim tells Samuel,
n we all follow him
back inside the cabin.

I'll keep watch,
Brooklyn calls after us.

Samuel gives Uncle Jim
a pillow stuffed
with cattail fluff.
Uncle Jim stretches out
on the fur rug.
Me n Willy crawl next to
Mama n Thomas,
both breathin heavy.
I don't hardly have time
to thank the good Lord
before I'm in a sleep
deeper'n any
I can remember.

When I wake up,
Mama's sittin
on the edge
of the bed,
jus watchin me.
A soft, gray darkness
is settlin in the room.

I didn't want you
to be afraid,
if you woke up
n we was gone.

Before we go outside,
I nestle into Mama's arms,
Mama, I whisper, *I'm sorry—*
I put everyone in danger—

We always been in danger.

Not like this, Mama!
What if a wildcat
gets hungry?
What if Will—

Mama hushes me.
We jus got to teach him
the ways of the woods.
We jus got to trust
the good Lord.

I snuggle closer.
I wish I could
trust the Lord
like Mama does,
but for now I trust
the arms what's holdin me.

Come outside,
Mama says.
Whatever tomorrow brings,
tonight we is here.
Tonight we is together.

Me n Mama hold hands
n stand in the dark room.
A single moonbeam is
shinin a path
what we follow
to the cabin door.

Outside, folks
we haven't met
is huddled round
a small fire.
Uncle Jim's holdin Thomas,
n Willy's sittin by his feet.
Mama n me stand beside em,
my legs not believin
they's standin still
while the moon's sendin
its purest light.

Two skinned rabbits
is curled on a stick,
roastin over the fire.
A man what reminds me
of Jordon is tellin a story.
Never would've run
if Master didn't
give me a gun
n tell me to kill Henry
for workin too slow.

A toothless man
with watery eyes
n a gray-n-white beard
interrupts.
I was workin hard as
these ole bones let me.

The man what reminds me
of Jordon continues.
Wanted me to shoot Henry
right there in the daylight,
right there with folks
pickin cotton
all round him.
Slow n steady—
like I was obeyin—
I walked to the field,
pointed the gun at Henry,
n told him
we both needed
to run.

Didn't think
these ole bones'd
carry me,
Henry says,
but Master's gun kept em
from followin us.
He shakes his head.
Still pinch myself,
to make sure
I really is free.

Maddie brings
Mama n me
gourds filled
with warm sweet tea
made from juniper berries.
I'll show you how
to smoke a hive
n gather honey,
she promises us.

Maddie tells us how
she toiled n sweated
in a tobacco field
till what afternoon
she saw Mary,
a woman spectin a baby,
gettin whipped
for no reason at all.
That night Samuel n me
made a plan
n we took Mary with us.
It wasn't easy
but we made it.

Maddie smiles n nods
at the smallest cabin
what's in the center
of the circle.
Mary's rockin Isaac now.

Nothin but joy that boy is—
strong. Beautiful.
Born in Freedom.

Seems everybody's
got a story to share.
But even more'n tellin,
they's listenin n
askin questions,
sadly wonderin bout
folks they left behind—
or children
what was torn away.

The gourd is warm
in my cupped hands

n I think bout Anna,
n her tremblin hands.

I never even said
good-bye.

We stay another day
with Samuel n Maddie
to learn bout survivin
in the swamp—
when's best to hide,
where's best to hunt,
what to do if a bear
crosses our path.

Then we move
to a small clearin
a mornin's walk
from the settlement.

Brooklyn travels with us
n helps dig a pit
deep as it is wide.
He helps us line it
with thin, dry stones
what won't pop
n crack when we cook.

He shows us
how to build a cabin
what's lifted off the ground
so it stays dry
when the rains come.

Most mornins, Uncle Jim
n Brooklyn hunt for birds

n squirrels.
Sometimes
they take Willy along,
n Brooklyn shows him
the hollowed logs
n burrows
where rabbits like to hide.
Thomas comes
with Mama n me
to gather berries.
Mama carries Thomas
n I carry the basket.
Every time Thomas
drops a berry in my basket,
he smiles a quiet smile
sweeter'n any berry
we gather.

In the afternoons,
Uncle Jim pounds the posts,
while Brooklyn
shows Mama n me
how to weave together
twigs n branches
for the floor, walls, n roof.
He shows us how to plait
marsh grass n palmetto leaves
to cover the cracks
n keep away
the wind n rain.

Nearby, the boys
draw pictures
or make mud cakes.

At night when we's takin
our rest neath the stars,
Brooklyn tells me
more of his story.

I stayed with my mama
till I was seven years old, he says.
We lived in a cabin with my daddy
and three little brothers.
One night my daddy escaped.
He told Mama
he'd find a job up north
and save enough money
to buy his Freedom—
and our Freedom too.
At night Mama told us
stories about how life would be
when we lived up north.

Brooklyn's voice is
soft n wistful as a loon's.

Only, my daddy
never came back
and that master—
the one who let Mama keep us
and tell us stories at night—
that master died
and his son brought all of us
to the auction block.
Brooklyn stops talkin,
n the night air
weighs heavy
with memories
n imaginins.

Finally Brooklyn speaks.
We were all sold
to different masters,
he says in a quiverin voice.
Sometimes at night,
I still hear Mama crying.

Was your new master cruel?
I ask.

Not in the beginning,
Brooklyn says.
I was a house slave—
but when I ran away
he whipped me
and made me
take care of the dogs
and sleep with them
on the floor of the barn.

Well, it's good you did
take care of em, I say,
rememberin how the dogs
let Brooklyn escape.
You beat him at his own game.

I think of Jordon
n his scratched hands,
n pray he found his way
to Freedom.

Sometimes Samuel
n one of the other men
from the settlement
come by to help lift logs
or make cement
from the mud
n crushed oyster shells
we gather from the bog.

We share what food we have,
n the men return
to the settlement.

Only Brooklyn stays with us.
On days they don't hunt,
him n Uncle Jim take the boys
to fish in the stream.
Sometimes Brooklyn stays behind
to show Mama n me
how to dry n pound cattail roots
to make flour
or how to boil em like taters.

But always at night,
restin neath the stars,
we whisper our stories.
I tell him bout Jordon
n his baby girl
he'll never see again.
I tell him bout Aunt Tempie

n Aunt Sara, Uncle Moses
n Anna,
bout Master Allen
n the Missus,
n her dishes what come
all the way from England,
n her bed
what's got a roof over it.

It's called a canopy bed,
Brooklyn says.
The master had one.

Brooklyn knows
lots of things I don't.
He even taught himself
to read by listenin
to his master's children
recitin they letters,
n watchin
his master's children
write they names.

It's confusing at first,
he says,
but I can teach you.

Now when we finish
buildin for the day,
when the squirrel's
been gutted

n the fish smoked,
when the dandelions
is crushed for coffee
or cut for soup,
we clear a space
to write letters in the dirt.

If Willy's nearby, he listens
n watches.
Brooklyn shows him the letter
what starts his name,
so sometimes a row
of upside-down mountains
circle Willy's pictures.

Willy n wagon n wheeeee,
Brooklyn says,
liftin Willy up
n spinnin him round.

Willy laughs,
but only softly,
like a bell
what's covered with feathers.

I sometimes wonder if Brooklyn's
thinkin of his own little brothers,
n feelin the same heavin sorrow
I felt when I moved to the Big House.

Finally our cabin's finished.
It's bigger'n the cabin
we left behind,
n lifted off the ground
with vine-n-log stairs
what sway when
we climb em
n a roof what looks like
a hat made of grass.

A giant cypress
stands guard out front.

First time we climb in,
Uncle Jim takes off his hat.
We all hold hands—
even Thomas n Willy—
n Mama thanks the good Lord
for keepin us safe.
Remember too,
she says,
Sara, OleGeorgeCooper,
n all the folks we left behind.

Brooklyn makes ready
to go back
to the settlement,
but Mama asks him
to stay.
The boys love you,

she says.
We all do—
n there's room here—
plenty of room.

I haven't even learned
all my letters yet, I say,
n feel my face boilin.

Uncle Jim puts his hand
on Brooklyn's shoulder.
I could use the help, son.

Well, sir, if Samuel—

Already asked him,
Uncle Jim says.
Only rule is,
you got to call me
Uncle Jim.

Tears fill Brooklyn's eyes,
but his smile's
wider'n the moon.

Well, sir—
I mean Uncle Jim—
then I accept.
Samuel and Maddie have
been good to me—

he lifts Thomas
into his arms—
but I sure do miss
havin brothers.

That night we all sleep
under one roof,
alert for the sounds
of wolves n wildcats,
but safe from
the lash of
the master's whip,
n sheltered by walls
made of palmetto leaves
n love.

A few weeks
after we finish
buildin our cabin,
I'm lyin in the dark
ponderin
n listenin
for wildcats
what might come
devour us.

I hear a soft
rustlin sound
n my heart
starts poundin
inside my head.

I sit up.

In the corner,
Uncle Jim
sleeps peacefully,
his homemade spear
on one side
n Mama
on the other.

I peek through
our grass wall.

Brooklyn sits alone
in the moonlight.

Careful I step
over Thomas
n slip outside.

What is you doin out here?
I ask, makin room for myself
on a molderin log.

Bove us,
a full moon sits
on the treetop
like a giant
white clover.
The air's moist n still.

Can't sleep,
Brooklyn says.
Lots of nights
I lie awake
wondering
where they are—
my mother and my brothers,
my father—
what happened to them?

They's somewhere, I say,
n I bet they's thinkin of you
every day.
The things what we love
we keep buried
in our hearts.

Brooklyn nods.
My brothers were little,

so maybe they'll forget.
But I won't, and I know
my mama and my daddy
won't forget either.

Each of us sit quiet,
ponderin the folks
what's buried
in our hearts.

How long have you been living
with Uncle Jim?
Brooklyn finally asks.

Bout five years.
Uncle Jim's the only father
I ever knowed.
I smile.
He'll take good care
of you too.

I think of Brooklyn
teachin himself to read,
escapin without a family
to give him hope n shelter.
Course it don't seem like you
need much carin for.

Everybody needs caring for,
Brooklyn says.

Specially white folks,
I say.
They can't do nothin
for emselves.

Swift as a feathered arrow,
I hear Aunt Tempie's voice
crossin the swamp to scold me.
Judgin folks by the color
of they skin is wrong—
no matter who's
doin' the judgin.

A snarlin snort n screech
what mus be
fightin raccoons
interrupts my thoughts,
but finally Brooklyn starts
talkin again.

Sometimes it feels
like my mama
never even existed.
Like I never existed.
Always hiding,
never leaving a trace
of who I am
or where I've been.
He buries his bare feet
in a mat of leaves.
It's like we don't exist.

I wish I could say somethin
to make Brooklyn feel better.
We exist same as the moon
n the stars,
I say.

Brooklyn shakes his head
n looks at me.
His eyes glisten
like the rainwater
what collects in
molderin leaves.

It doesn't matter, Grace.
No one will remember us.
No one will even know
we were here.

Master Allen thought
Aunt Sara was useless.
Thought she wouldn't
bring in gullyfluff.

But Master Allen
was wrong.

Aunt Sara matters.
She knows things.
She knows how to keep
boys quiet
with dirt drawins
n broken buttons.
She knows to step away
from a snake
what's got poison in him.

Aunt Tempie matters too.
I feel a stab of sorrow
for how I misjudged her.
I wonder how many folks
she saved with her ham patties
n johnnycakes,
with her secret messages
scratched into rocks.

Jordon n Uncle Moses—
they matter too—
n no one works harder'n

poor Anna—
the Missus don't know it—
but Anna matters.
Even Thomas—
what don't do nothin
but give sweet smiles—
he matters.

Everyone's got a way of matterin.

The only thing
what *don't* matter
is what color
the good Lord paints us.

Come with me, I say.
I grab Brooklyn's hand,
pull him to the cypress
what guards our cabin,
n kneel down.

What are you doing?
Brooklyn asks.

Shhhh, I say,
help me clear away these leaves.

We clear a space.
With a sharp rock,
I dig a hole,
small n deep as my fist.

I pull Aunt Sara's
porcelain button
from my pocket.

Squeeze this, I whisper.

Brooklyn takes the button.

Now close your eyes
n repeat what I say.

I take a deep breath
n start talkin.

My name is Brooklyn.
I have a scar on my face
from bein struck
by my master's cane.
I walk with a limp
from the whippin I got
first time I ran away.

Brooklyn squeezes
the button
n repeats my words.

Master thought I was stupid,
I continue,
but I taught myself to read.
I know all what plants is good
n all what plants is poison.
I know how to build a house.

Again Brooklyn repeats
my words,
not even changin em
to make em sound
more like him.

Now it's your turn, he says.
Tell your story.

I take the button
n squeeze it.

My name is Grace.
I know what's right
n what's wrong,
n I know keepin slaves
is wrong.
Bindin folks in chains
n sellin em
like they's nothin more'n
dried tobacco
is wrong.
Makin em
sleep on the floor,
bringin em
to the smokehouse
n whippin em,
ballyraggin so they's
too scared to breathe
is wrong, wrong, wrong.

My heart swells with rightiness,
n I squeeze my fingers tighter
round the button.

Stealin children,
makin em work
till they bones
is weak as jelly,
bindin they
thoughts
n words,
forcin em

to flee
n kill snakes
n eat lizards
is wrong.
There's nobody
ever can blame us
for wantin
to be free.
The good Lord
made this big,
beautiful world
for everybody.

I wind a strand of hair
round my finger n pluck it.
Brooklyn watches me
n does the same.

We wrap the strands
round the button,
bury the button,
n cover up the hole.

Anyone ever finds this
will know we existed,
I say,
will know we was here,
will know we mattered—
n didn't belong
to nobody but ourselves.

Though they stay skinny
n light as swamp grass
n never wander
beyond the trees
what surround our cabin,
Thomas n Willy
grow stronger.

They play hide-n-seek,
wobble on stick stilts,
n make silly faces.
They laugh,
but never very loud.
They don't hardly even speak
bove a whisper.

One mornin Thomas steps
on a rat's nest n gets bit
in three places.
Three large, red swellins
appear on his foot.
He whimpers like a kitten
but don't scream.

How come he's not hollerin?
I ask Mama.

Fear chokes the warble
from some birds
n never gives it back,

Mama says, chewin
the plant Maddie
says is good for bites
n pattin it on Thomas's foot.

When the good Lord's done
washin away
OleGeorgeCooper's scars
n wipin away the scar
what slashes
Brooklyn's brow,
I hope He has time
to give little boy voices
back to Thomas n Willy.

One mornin,
when the three-petaled flowers
is burstin through the thicket
n lacy-winged dragonflies
is dartin n droppin
bove rain puddles,
Brooklyn n me venture out
to gather mushrooms.

I hear a rustle
in the tree bove us,
n I jump.

*Just a yellow warbler
going home,*
Brooklyn laughs

n I laugh too.

We don't ever
let our guard down,
but it's good to be out
in the daytime,
good to laugh
n to learn things
I never even
wondered bout.

I know how
to tell what plants is safe

n what plants is poison.
I know how
to coil swamp grass
into baskets
what can hold water
n how to burn pine branches
to smoke away the honeybees
n gather honey.
I know how to peel
n hone sticks
to make em sharp enough
to gut a fish
n how to make bowls by
soakin n cuttin dry gourds.
I know all my letters,
n even how to scratch out
some words.

My favorite word
is *FREEDOM*.

I wish I could tell
Aunt Sara n Aunt Tempie
I finally understand.

Freedom's not jus a place
you find on a map.

Freedom's livin
with folks who love you
n havin the space
to love yourself.

Freedom's not bein afraid
to say your own thoughts
n follow your own heart,
jus like the good Lord intended.

This fine mornin,
under this blue sky
with a tiny yellow warbler
singin fearless in the trees,

I know I'm free.

I'm free
n I'm never
goin to be
not free again.

The Great Dismal Swamp is a real place—a large marshy area spanning parts of Virginia and North Carolina—and I was fortunate to stumble into it while researching another idea for a story. What I discovered in this inhospitable wilderness surprised and inspired me.

By the early 1860s, when my story takes place, Native Americans had been living in the Great Dismal Swamp for thousands of years. Some had naturally migrated there; others sought to escape the tyranny and encroachment of European settlers. What I didn't know was that the swamp was also a refuge for enslaved people seeking freedom. These wilderness runaways were called maroons. Those who settled at the edge of the swamp, close to civilization, were called border maroons, and they received food and supplies in secret from nearby farms and plantations. Those who settled farther away (as I imagined Grace and her family did), in a deeply secluded area of the interior swamp, were called hinterland maroons. Hinterland maroons were self-sufficient, built their own shelters, foraged for their food, and lived lives independent of the society that had enslaved them.

Because a maroon's survival depended on secrecy, and because mud-and-wood homes disintegrate and decay, it is not easy to determine how many individuals forged their freedom in the Great Dismal Swamp. Life in the wilderness was difficult. Some maroons were caught and killed before they reached safety. Those who were not caught faced hunger, ferocious animals, and the extreme perils of living in the wild. Still, an untold number of maroons were able to survive in the swamplands. The choice to brave the wilderness rather than suffer the brutality and humiliation of bondage is a towering testimony to the spirit and conviction of an oppressed people who risked everything for the chance to be free.

ACKNOWLEDGMENTS

Although *Unbound* is a work of fiction, the imagined lives of Grace and her family are based on the experiences of real people. From 1936 to 1938, narratives of the formerly enslaved were prepared by the Federal Writers' Project. These first-person narratives painfully recount the cruelty inherent in any system that allows one individual power over another. The photographs and memories shared by the Federal Writers' Project were an indispensable research tool as I pieced together the circumstances of Grace's life and tried to evoke authentic voices of the time.

An NPR article, "Fleeing to Dismal Swamp, Slaves and Outcasts Found Freedom," describing the work of Dr. Daniel O. Sayers (Department of Anthropology, American University) was my first introduction to the maroons. The untold stories behind the tiny artifacts found by Sayers and his team first set me on my journey to the Great Dismal Swamp.

I am most grateful to Dr. Sylviane A. Diouf, Director of the Lapidus Center for the Historical Analysis of Transatlantic Slavery at the Schomburg Center for Research in Black Culture, for her in-depth exploration of maroon society in *Slavery's Exiles: The Story of the American Maroons* (New York University Press, 2014). Her research helped me navigate the swamp and imagine what life for these exiles must have been like. I would also like to thank Dr. Diouf for her detailed reading and sensitive suggestions when fact-checking my manuscript. Her knowledge, insights, and expertise were invaluable.

As always, I owe a wealth of gratitude to my editor, Tracy Mack, who encouraged me to dig, forage, and find the forgotten voices of the swamp. Tracy's continual support and profound sensitivity have given me the confidence to explore and create. I am grateful for her guidance and know how very much this book has been enriched by her understanding and intuition.

Thanks to Christopher Silas Neal for his beautiful and evocative cover art. Many thanks to Tracy's assistant, Kait Feldmann; copyeditor, Anne Heausler; proofreader, Joy Simpkins; art director, Marijka Kostiw; library marketing director, Lizette Serrano; and the wonderful Scholastic team. Thanks also to my agent, Jodi Reamer. I am grateful for the time and effort each of you has dedicated to this project.

Most of all, thanks to my family—Marc, Alex, Celia, and Ben—who lovingly and patiently accept my constant clutter of paper and books. I am also grateful for my cherished extended family—the Marottas, the Burgs, and the Schieffelins. Because of them I could more acutely imagine the crushing anguish that people who were enslaved must have endured when forced to separate from the families they loved.

FOR
MARC, ALEX,
CELIA, AND BEN,
AND FOR VOICES
UNHEARD OR
FORGOTTEN

Copyright © 2018 by Ann E. Burg

All rights reserved. Published by Scholastic Inc., *Publishers since 1920*. SCHOLASTIC,
SCHOLASTIC PRESS, and associated logos are trademarks and/or registered trademarks of Scholastic Inc.

The publisher does not have any control over and does not assume any responsibility for author or
third-party websites or their content.

No part of this publication may be reproduced, stored in a retrieval system, or transmitted in any form or by
any means, electronic, mechanical, photocopying, recording, or otherwise, without written permission of the
publisher. For information regarding permission, write to Scholastic Inc., Attention: Permissions Department,
557 Broadway, New York, NY 10012.

This book is a work of fiction. Names, characters, places, and incidents are either the product of the author's
imagination or are used fictitiously, and any resemblance to actual persons, living or dead,
business establishments, events, or locales is entirely coincidental.

ISBN 978-1-338-28208-5

12 11   21 22
Printed in the U.S.A.   40

This book was originally published in hardcover by Scholastic Press in 2016.
This edition first printing 2018

The text was set in Adobe Garamond Pro.
The jacket type was hand-lettered by Christopher Silas Neal.
The display type was set in Adobe Garamond Pro.
Book design by Marijka Kostiw